Orts:

Stories, Essays, And Things So Short They May Be Poems

Rich Cresswell

Copyright © 2013 by Rich Cresswell.
All rights reserved. This book or any portion thereof may not be reproduced or used in any manner whatsoever without the express written permission of the author except for the use of brief quotations in a book review.

First Printing, 2013
ISBN-13: 978-1492344513
ISBN-10: 1492344516

Ort: /ɔrt/

*Noun: a scrap or morsel of food left at a meal.
Origin:
1400–50; late Middle English*

A Word of Introduction.
(Or Perhaps Several Hundred of Them.)

When I was a kid, I hated the night. From the posters on my walls to the tree branch scratching at the window, everything seemed a potential source of terror. It's often been referred to as an over-active imagination. I don't know if that's exactly what it was.

Regardless, at some point I became counter-phobic enough that now, when it's dark, when everyone else is sleeping and there's nothing to distract me, the thoughts come clearly. The impulses to create or take action become immediate and insistent. In fact, it's usually in the last few moments of consciousness that I get up the energy to do something. In the daylight, things seem too intimidating, threatening. Things seem too difficult, like mountains. But somehow in the blackness and comfort of dark, you can only see the step directly ahead of you.

I just had the urge to get up and write an introduction, so I did. And hopefully, at some point,

I'll be able to fall back asleep. But for now, here's this.

When I started writing, I had no idea what I was doing. I had never taken a creative writing course. I had never written anything aside from what was required of me by classes and assignments. In 2008, I decided it might be fun to write fiction, and I gave myself the assignment of writing something every day. These short pieces I jokingly — or self-convincingly — referred to as exercises, but what they are actually the first steps of a toddler. They're clumsy. They're often silly. And I love them dearly.

Most of them deal with an issue that still bothers me to this day. We live in a world that is increasingly disconnected while things compete for our attention from every direction. We are animals who have convinced ourselves through the trappings and veneers of society that we are robots. That is the belief at the heart of the first section of this book, which deals with the interactions between things man and things man-made.

Many of the entries in this book revolve around this problem. I had initially written an introduction that would go through each section piece by piece, explaining and illuminating the motivations and themes. But that is at best foolish and at worst abjectly stupid. The only other one that should elicit explanation is the ninth, in which I spill my guts all over the page for all to see. All I ask is that you be gentle if you ever discuss it with me.

The idea for this book came from a prayer. Perhaps meditation or a dissociative episode, whatever you want to call it depending on your world-view. I was lying in bed one night, breathing deeply and trying my best to relax, going along with some mindfulness training that had been recommended to me for anxiety-reduction. I decided, in that moment of sheer desperation or brilliance — the difference is in presence or hindsight — that I should ask the universe a question. So I said, simply, "What do you want from me?"

The reply I received was a very warm, inclusive, "Nothing." It was not nothing in the sense of get out of here, it was nothing in the sense that you're fine, and you shouldn't worry about it. So I thought to myself about what I should be doing. I'd been trying to get together a creative endeavor and live a real life. Fully self-actualize or whatever term of the moment happens to be when you are reading this. I asked what to do, mumbled half-aloud, and was granted a vision.

Again, I do not claim this was a religious experience. For if it was, without a doubt, what came next was the most banal religious experience ever recorded. On the screen of the back of my closed eyelids, I saw a computer display. Specifically, multiple word processor windows and an Internet browser. I saw the things I had written, the place I had put them — where I knew, thanks to easily accessed search engine statistics, that probably about twelve people had ever read them. And so I began to assemble them, rewrite them. Build something real.

The reality, at its base, is that this book contains the first honesties spoken in the life of a long-suffering liar — The suffering, it should be noted, is a direct result of lying. Don't do it. That's probably sound advice — At any rate, this is a frightening experience. I am attempting to get a handle on things that occur in my head. I hope to get a grip on the great power that comes from articulating things, especially these things later in the book that are deep within myself but I have not given the courtesy of recognition until the past year or so.

    The lucky thing of course is that all of these issues which I have now finally been able to give voice to have existed for years. So even in those meandering first steps of 2008, I am able to recognize myself. As I traced back, editing and re-writing, I found a breadcrumb trail of my former beliefs. Many of these have now crystallized and become clearer, and many have been shed like so much dry elbow skin. Regardless, all along the way, I found bits of myself. Scraps of myself.

    Orts.

2:14 AM
Queens, NY
September 2013

I

Man and Man-Made

It has existed since fist met rock,
This dichotomous relationship.
It builds us, heals us,
Harms us and cleaves us.
Leaving us better and alone.

Bite The Bullet

Lawrence never was particularly good at understanding metaphors. But he certainly did do something he wasn't looking forward to that day. He may have been too dim to understand his boss' instructions about accepting the inevitable, but managed to make himself much more interesting in the process. Though it cost him his ability to eat solid food, speak clearly, and keep from horrifying children, he would always write on his miniature whiteboard (that's how he communicated afterwards) that he didn't regret it.

"Except for one thing," he would scrawl, with mischief in his hazy, drooping eye.

"The taste."

The High Iron

"Just think," John said, ignoring the glittering cityscape behind in favor of the dull metal before him, "One day, this beam will be buried. It will be no more real to the people who work here than a man's skull is when you look at his face."

He paused, wincing into the sunlight as a bird flew past.

"Structure's a funny thing. You never know you had it til it's gone."

The Frowning Banana

As most are, his new diet is based on shame. However, he has elected to take a direct, externalized approach. Rather than rely on self-shaming—and in so doing accept responsibility for his consumption—he makes food do the work for him. "If this doesn't work," he thinks to himself, "I can always get chickens. I couldn't kill a chicken."

What he doesn't know is that he's fooling himself. Doing more work than necessary to achieve his goal. But life, when not complicated by illusions of debt to inanimate objects, seems hopeless. Difficult.

He puts down the fast food container and lifts one greasy finger to his mouth, licking tiny granules of salt from under the nail. His other hand reaches for the marker. "This has got to work. There's simply no other way."

"Cannibal Sacrifice: Inquire Within"

All in all, the cult wasn't going well. Jake worked tirelessly, but his ads in the local paper met with little response. Most of the people who showed up for his meetings were trying to sell him vacuum cleaners or timeshares. He'd had enough.

It occurred to him one night that maybe there just wasn't room in the world for any more ideas. Maybe the brains of his so-called fellow men were just plain filled with potential facts. He was, after all, in a race. Marx had speculated rightly that the world was full of competing ideologies. A marketplace of truths. What he needed was blatant falsehood. For lack of a better term: something stupid.

The sign had been up for under an hour when a van of college kids pulled into his driveway. Jake donned the purple robe that had been hanging in his closet for weeks and answered the doorbell. He had to fight to keep a straight face.

The Golden Record

They sent it with the best intentions. Humanity's beacon and representative. An inanimate testimony to the triumphs of our race. They never truly expected a response.

The response was mixed, at best. Universally, humans were accepted, but with the begrudging sigh of an older brother ordered to take his younger sibling with him on a trip into the woods. We were trouble. They knew it.

They never attacked, and never hid from us. They never played cruel tricks. And that was the worst part. They saw what we were, and they simply accepted it. Quietly.

The Golden Record, received and read, was little more than the innocent scrawl of a child. Scratching the bare surface of the universe. They sent back a greeting. A welcome to the community. And then stared as we jumped and raved, jabbered and shook with anticipation.

They visited occasionally. And found little they understood, let alone were interested in.

When they were done with the record, they added a great outer disc and shot it further out into the void. A chain letter of evolving intelligence. They sent it with the best intentions. An inanimate testimony to the triumphs of their race, surrounding our own — their discovery. Their property. They never truly expected a response.

Skyscrapers and Canopies

In the most ancient of days, ages before the birth of Christ (arguably the most famous individual in present awareness), we were essentially the same.

We spent hard-working days in the sun and hunted and gathered. We slept in treetops to avoid predation and descended, each morning a gift, to forage for edible plants and catch the odd possum or two.

At present, we do little differently. After all, we operate using the same bodily machinery as the emergent homo sapiens of fifty thousand years ago.

Each night we ascend to some place of security, viewing the dark streets as dangerous. Our muggers and rapists were their saber-toothed tigers. To us, the night is still wilderness.

So, as technology advanced, we built ever upwards. Trying to run from ground level. From the lurking cat or hissing snake. From things we are evolutionarily conditioned to be afraid of. We didn't evolve as such; we just built bigger and bigger trees.

All over the world, humans now rest, in some places a thousand feet above the ground or more. Each morning, they perform the ritual descent into the (relative) safety of morning. Find food. Do work.

Repeat.

Technology has done nothing to speed up humanity. It has merely complicated it. What was once picking berries is now building a machine that can core two tons of apples a day. We've moved from the early beginnings of domesticating animals to the early stages of manufacturing them.
We celebrate our genius. We celebrate our triumphs. The engines, the light bulbs, the copper wire which powers them.

But each night, we come home and climb our tree. Settle into the bedding, and feel secure. Not because we've eradicated them, but because we've found a better way to distance ourselves from them. Sleep. Height. Security. All synonyms to our ancient brains and their modern counterparts.

Vines, Roots, Pills

The explorers stared into the rainforest, from the edge of a hazy clifftop. They looked below and saw lush jungle spread before them. The dark greens of vigorous trees and bright splashes of flowering plants. Animals moved about, shaking the tops of trees hundreds of years old.

The explorers saw resources, but not in a way that they could've understood. They cut into the wood, mined the surrounding hills. Took wood and rocks while true wealth escaped them. The natives spoke out, showing them leaves that would help in high altitudes, roots that alleviated pain. They took these all as paltry substitutes for the sophisticated tinctures of home.

Their grandchildren were the first to discover the essence of each plant. They learned that they could distill the mass, holistic effect of a given vegetable and condense it into a capsule.

Everything was broken down. Simplified. The whole became a sum of parts, and the pertinent parts transformed into more easily accessible forms. The whole was no longer important. Digestible resources that fit in your hand. That make you better. Supplements, vitamins, drugs.

The explorers wouldn't have understood. Their grandchildren saw dollar signs in the tiny components of leaves and sticks, rather than gems and fuel.

Two generations further removed, the great-great grandchildren of the explorers fight for the rainforest, fight for whole plants and ecosystems. The focus is back to macro. But still, the grocery store shelves are filled with bottles. Each promising positive effects. The condensed materials of a once mighty forest. An impenetrable mystery bottled and sold.

Morning Ritual

The shaman rises early, as we all must in times of need. He passes the gently breathing bodies of the boys who will become men this day, padding softly on the earthen floor of the long house.

Outside the air is damp, redolent with fertility. Insects hum and buzz about him as he nears the sacred grove. The plants he seeks.

He pulls a handful of vines towards him, slicing them with a homemade blade. Then he kneels at the other side of the clearing, spreading the earth away from the bitter root he requires.

He returns home and places a clay pot amidst the smoldering coals of last night's fire. He adds the mashed root and pours water over it. A dark, herbal smell arises as the water hisses on heated clay.

The vines are stripped and dropped into the cauldron, where they will boil until evening. He sits over the brew, eyes closed, and hums the quiet songs of other worlds. Songs he learned on his own journey into manhood, many years ago. The songs the plants taught him to sing.

A world away, you wake, bleary. You ease out of bed, fearful of light and sound. You open the freezer and pop a plastic lid from a tin can as water boils on the stove.

The grounds turn to hot mud in the filter, and concentrated alertness drips quietly into the cup, breaking the morning silence. You begin to feel better about the day to come.

Intentional or not, ritual is ritual.

Training the Dogs

Before he got into this line of work, Michael had been fooling himself.

He'd been convinced that domestication was irreversible. Foolproof. Bad dogs were simply poorly trained. As a boy, he frowned and cringed at pitbulls in the park, throats straining at leashes. Their bodies were tightly wound coils of muscle, poised at a child's height.

When he got his job, Michael knew there would be work to do. Taking a well-trained animal and regressing it to its baser instincts.

Each morning, he'd don the padded suit and think to himself: "We just have to open that door. Let out the beast living deep inside our buddies."

Within a week, he knew the truth. Opening the door was the easy part. The real trick, as had never been done with the pitbulls he remembered from his youth, was keeping that door closed the vast majority of the time.

"I've made a mistake," he'd think as his body was dragged to the ground. "We have to find our buddies somewhere inside these beasts."

A flash of teeth, the smell of wet breath through the facemask. Then a release. And relief. "My friend is back," he would think.

And every time, he was surprised.

Alligator Kisses

Displays of affection are rare in the animal kingdom. Humanity fawns over one another, provides constant reminders of tenderness and intimacy.

In the cold-blooded world, it is often the shifting of a fish from one's teeth to the mouth of one's partner. Sharing is universal. As is mating.

But, from time to time, the exchange of body heat occurs without the exchange of bodily fluid.

They bask on the shore, heads nestled together, sharing secret thoughts. They have food and drink. Their offspring are successful and plentiful. They have eliminated most threats.

They've found each other, and found a rare moment of calm. A quiet window of primeval happiness. Sated stomachs and no immediate threats. They bask and purr, skin on skin.

Rain Dance

All across the valley, the water had dried up. For miles, dusty riverbeds traced a road map of thirst across a sallow landscape. The animals began looking to the heavens, one by one, aching to see the dark of clouds obscure an unforgiving sun.

It was only a matter of time before they began to pray.

It's natural, as odd as it seems, to seek aid from those more powerful than ourselves.

The difference between the cry of an infant and the clasped hands and closed eyes of the faithful is measured only by demonstrable success rate.

They gathered in circles, crouching on tails and haunches, raising whiskered faces to the sky. On the fourth day of their meeting, the stark azure above relented.

A single drop fell, thudding to the earth and turning dust to mud. They held their vigil, struck in the face by tiny beads of life itself.

Prayers are answered, in time. Whether by chance or by the agency of some unknowable being. That's what keeps them seeking the aid of those above. Each dry season, they gather, claws and paws clasped in silence, the food chain broken by a common need.

At the end of each season, their prayers are answered, and life goes back to normal.

II

Future's Past

*We are not, as we so often think,
The crest of the wave.
We are rather
The undertow.
Drawing the next generation back
Then hurling it forwards
To a set of foregone conclusions.*

May 21st, 2011

If one man is right, the world is now forever changed. The good and plentiful have been Raptured off to wherever it is they go, and the remainders are the scum, the uncertain. Certainty (faith) has greater value than ever these days. It could well be your get-out-of-this-painful-existence free card.

If one man is right, the streets are half empty. Maybe less. Piles of shoes and clothing left behind. Piles of humans left behind to ponder the meaning of it all. To rue their doubt and rage against their parents for giving them the wrong upbringing. The anger it will unleash.

If one man is right, my readership is now lessened. Possibly. I'm not really sure who's reading this.

If one man is right, today is a great day of change. Today is a day when the world must be fought for, where lines will be drawn and battles will commence. And where life, as we know it, is no longer life as we know it.

If one man is right, today marks the beginning of a new normal.

The problem is that truth is consensus. Reality agreed upon. No one has yet — or recently, depending on what you believe — attained a pure knowledge pipeline to whatever mystic beings lie beyond our reach. So we all mill around, agreeing that words mean this and that up is that way, et cetera et cetera ad nauseam.

If one man is right, about something so impossibly large and knowable, then I'd rather be left behind. To continue milling and debating, figuring out the world as it flies by us. The answers bore me. As do the people who claim to have them.

Is it wrong of me to hope that one man is right?

Light Poles and WiFi

The messages fly overhead, zipping along fiber optics and copper. Translated into electrical impulses, the workings of the modern world are all around us. Radio waves pulse through your body; cell phones use your car as an antenna.

A wealth of information, tuned to a different frequency than our eyes. If we saw it, it would be blinding. If we were to catch a glimpse, it would mean madness.

A man, somewhere bland and flat, has tuned into this. He has learned to read the codes which permeate our atmosphere. He finds it hard to leave the house, each time inundated by innumerable colors and a cacophony of communications.

He sits in his living room and patiently constructs.

He is meticulous. He twists the ends of chicken wire through holes he drilled in metal frames. He welds the frames together, creating canvasses of interference. He insulates himself. He read about Faraday's experiments on Wikipedia, and knew it was the only solution to his unique problem.

So he sits at home, building to regain the emptiness and silence we sometimes dread. The quiet night, the clear sky.

He builds a cage around himself, so he can finally feel the freedom we take for granted.

The Vault

"What do you mean, a hundred years!?" The question erupted from her mouth, echoing through the underground chamber.

"I told you. It's the only way to be sure," came his reply. His voice, normally hoarse and tentative, seemed to boom in the enclosed space.

"But you don't know what's out there! You don't know how things will turn out. It might be fine tomorrow. They might survive!"

"It doesn't matter. It's done. Whether the sun comes up tomorrow or not."

"Of course the sun will come--" she paused. A cracking sound escaped her throat, her eyes bright with tears in the near-darkness. "I won't see it." A sob. "I won't ever."

"But you'll live." He reached out to touch her shoulder.

She stumbled to the corner, shoulder rubbing cold metal as she slumped down the wall. He stood and watched, chewing his lip and regretting the high price of safety.

Walkers and Epees

As human lifespan increased towards the end of the 21st century, so did an interest in sporting activities of yore. Previously archaic forms of mock-battle were brought back to the fore as people whiled away their later years. They were thirsty for adventure. Craving action.

The bodies, withered and shrunken, took up edgeless blades and guns modified to fire electrostatic pellets. Dueling became one of the most popular activities in the 100+ age range, provided contestants proved healthy enough to endure the stinging shock of the pellets. Liver-spotted hands grasped handles. Wheeled themselves out to twenty paces. Turned and fired.

One would fall, twitching slightly in the dust. The other would mockingly blow imagined smoke from the barrel off their pistol, squinting into the sun. They would think, "I am bad. I can beat others. I am strong." Great-great-grandfather: a gunslinger. The Millennial Generation never outgrew escapism.

Beautiful Plumage.

At the advent of the 22nd century, Geneto-Splicing™ provided untold dimensions of variability in the world of popular culture. Accessories grew directly from the skin of models, and animal traits were bred into humans to accomplish specific tasks. The military experimented with baboon hindquarters and muzzles, giving their soldiers an unmatched vertical leap and weaponless killing capabilities. In the civilian sector, these scientific leaps were applied foremost to fashion, but humanitarian uses soon became apparent.

New York City was hit particularly hard in the spring of 2116, when the homeless shed the downy coats gifted to them by the Genesoft Foundation. It cost taxpayers an estimated 84 million in additional street-cleaning vehicles. When reached for comment, a Genesoft spokesthing asked, "Would it be better to let them freeze? To return to nature's cruel process of selection? Nature has not been involved in our affairs for some time. Why bring it back now?"

III

Mental Health

This way madness lies.
Indeed.
In all these ways,
In each our own,
We express these newfound plagues.

Obsessive Compulsions

Everything is in order in Mr. Nelson's little world. His plot of earth is ringed by a perfect square of boxwood, shaved level across the top. His dogs trimmed into poofs of white hair, elongated bare limbs stretching down to tufted feet. Mr. Nelson maintains it all with a great deal of labor, but it is truly a labor of love.

Or at least, a labor of need.

He walks outside and finds a single, gnarled twig out of place. Amiss. His heartbeat flares. His face goes flush and the rushing sound of a thousand insects fills his ears. In an instant, he flees the scene and shoves the garage door open, shouldering through into the dank space. Pulling the cord of an overhead light, he examines his tools, hanging outlined on pegboard. He removes the shears, leaving their outline bare and conspicuous as the site of a death.

He runs back to the hedging, verging on tears

as he squats, careful to pull his khakis up out of the loam.

He centers the shears around the errant branch, steadying his right wrist with his left hand. He takes a deep breath once. Twice. And snip. His fingers come together as his eyes squeeze shut.

An inch of green wood and four leaves fall to the ground. And all is well again. Mr. Nelson stands and removes his glasses. He wipes them on his blue Oxford shirt and exhales deeply, trying to let the need escape him with the air. Try as he might, it never quite makes it.

Narcissism

"They call it Peter Pan Syndrome," he says disdainfully. Smoke curls out from his nostrils, a dragon in bright athletic gear. He sermonizes from a cushy leather couch in one of his three living rooms. "They say I don't want to grow up. But that's not really what it is."

"Do you mind if I ask what it is?" The interviewer is meek, pressed trousers and black, plastic-rimmed glasses. He's the picture of geek chic, interviewing a man too wealthy to notice the appearance of others.

"Well, it's simple really. It's replacement. It's a late replacement."

"You mean it makes up for the things you lacked earlier in life?"

"Yeah. Exactly. Except I'm bigger now, so it has to be bigger."

The interviewer isn't sure what to say. He pauses, pen hanging above his pad of paper, silence running into the mp3 recorder lying on the table. The red light stares at him accusingly.

"Listen, man. You want an explanation?"

The interviewer nods.

"Say you find a guy, a regular Joe. Just some poor asshole who's worked his whole life to scrounge up enough dough to feed his family, put his kids through school, make house and car payments. You go to him and you ask him to think back, deep in his childhood," another inhalation and exhalation of smoke. The air is rank with the smell of ash. "You go to him and you say, 'Hey man, what was the one thing you always wanted? The one thing you always wanted but your parents would never get you? What was missing?' And he'd look at you and think for a minute and maybe say a tricycle or an action figure or some other thing. Now say you go out, and you find that exact thing. The exact wish he had when he was a kid. And you track this guy down and you find him leaving the store he works in or the warehouse where he mops the floor... And you give it to him. What do you think he's going to do?"

"I really don't know."

"He's going to laugh in your fucking face and keep on walking. Because what good is a goddamn tricycle when you've got bills to pay and work to do. These things: toys and games, nonsense. They were big when we were little. Now we're big and they're the small ones. So you have to make them bigger. Better. Tricycles become cars with 22" rims, action figures and dolls become bodyguards and groupies. But only if you've got the money to get them. And I do. So yeah, to answer your original question: I have grown up, I just have the means to do what we all want to do."

The Concrete Child

He sees the world in black and white. "Mom" and "Dad" are more ideas than they are identifiers. Two larger, adult humans who care for him and meet some of his needs. He sees their faces as individual features, moving in a complex symphony he lacks the vocabulary to understand. He recognizes his own features in the arch of his father's brow, but misses the twinkle in the eye below it. He doesn't understand his attachment to these people.
For now, he's a small boy, pressing the backs of his hands into his eyes. Pressing and pressing until he sees stars appear. A noise startles him and he looks up, seeing "Dad" enter the room. His teeth are showing. His eyes gentle. The boy ignores him and goes back to tracking those stars inside his eyes as they float across the room, always escaping his vision.

"Dad" stands and stares, trying to hide his disappointment. His frustration. He gets down on his knees, mere feet from the boy, whose eyes are still tracing arcs across the baby blue walls.

Later in life, he'll struggle to comprehend his peers. He'll feel little for anyone else but profound disconnection from them. Ostracized as much by his own mind as by their social cliques.

His father's been warned, by doctors and friends and helpful strangers. Each intrudes into his son's life, predicting various outcomes with differing levels of optimism. None of that matters right now. He stares at his son's eyes, waiting for connection between the two of them. Waiting for whatever thing separating them to lift.

Waiting for the stars to go out.

Paranoia

Old Jack was the star of this movie, and he'd never forgive the world for that. He would stand, crinkled notebook in hand, on street corners. Praying someone would notice. Praying that someone would realize they were the audience, and give him a chance to be heard.

It was a hard life, and it showed on his face. Veins glowed red beneath the crinkled leather of the skin on his nose. No one would believe him.

But he knew the truth. He knew the whole shebang. And he had written it down, painstakingly detailing the plot. Once he saw one of their agents standing on a street corner and he had to hide his notes for three days, tucked into the waistband of his filthy pants along with newspapers. It was finally safe again and he opened it in a park. He took a pencil he'd stolen from a drug store and began to scrawl:

"Close call. Too close. They're onto me. Why did I have to know? What did I do? The men will come soon.

"They'll come with knives and guns and nets and they'll take me. They'll take me away for tests and probes and elimination."

That was what "they" called it. "Elimination." Such a polite term, but mechanical—as was their way. He'd lost three friends fall elimination. Faked overdoses or trumped up arrests. Old Jack wasn't going out that easy. He'd move, each night, to a new place. People called him homeless, but he had a new home every night.

And every morning, he'd wake with the sun, and begin taking his notes again. Recording the plot everyone was missing. The faceless masses averted their eyes and wrinkling their noses as they passed him by, the occasional tourist giving him a quarter. It was hiding in plain sight. It was the best way for him to escape. The only way to survive.

Depression

His eyes slowly open, the brightness of day shocking him. What day is it? He's not sure. The clock stares at him, red digits glaring 11:31AM. He would have just overslept, in his old life.

Daniel sits up and slings his sore legs over the edge of the bed. He's always so tired nowadays. It's been nearly a month since he was "downsized" and he's been feeling worse lately. His job was stressful. Finance, business... Worrying about other people's money all the time. But now he has nothing to do but worry about himself.

His wife's been up for hours. Out doing the shopping, then going to her own job. His knees creak as he stands and staggers towards the door, passing the full-length mirror on the wall. Has he gotten fatter? Dark rings surround his eyes, stubble verging on a beard covers him from neck to cheek.

Daniel thinks he looks unhealthy. He feels unhealthy.

He moves into the kitchen and sees a newspaper folded neatly into quarters. His wife left it there, the classifieds with four ads circled in orange highlighter. He chokes down a sob of resentment and tries to analyze himself. Why is he so angry? Because there's no point. The next job will end too. The economy's in shambles, his life is just part of that. The situation is out of his control.

He stumbles to the shower and lets the steaming jet pour over his head and shoulders, elbows pressed against the cool tiles. Tears mix with the water trickling down his face, and he feels glad for a moment. For the release. He wishes he could stay in here all day. His stomach knots as he realizes: he could.

Attention Deficit

I walk down the tree-lined street and the sun shines through making animal shapes on the sidewalk, and then a bus goes by filled with children, their screams and smiling faces poking out through the thin windows which won't open enough for them to possibly fall out of because that's dangerous just like the window-washers above me washing the windows of offices where businessmen work and exchange cards with half-hearted fake handshakes and plastered on smiles in their suits that cost as much as the janitor makes sweeping up the hard tile floor that hurts like a bitch if you slip and bang your tailbone, like the skateboarding kid up ahead just did but wouldn't have if he'd been watching out for traffic, the constant stream of traffic that rumbles past on the avenue ahead where people mill slowly towards no particular destination floating in and out of every storefront and examining electronics, t-shirts, and cheap crap designed to be sold to tourists who ought to have picked a better place to visit like Myanmar or Mexico although it's dangerous to go to Mexico nowadays maybe even more dangerous than falling out of one of those high skyscraper windows that glint down at me like the shiny cobalt barrel of a gun, which they have lots of in Mexico and that's part of the problem, also the drugs which make their way up past the border and wind up in the hands of people like the shivering homeless guy on the corner who smells just like the Port-a-John at summer camp when I was a kid, old and crusted and probably rotting, a smell like dry leaves moldering in a gutter mixed with a foulness only humans can have, the trees don't produce the same smell no matter how rotten they get but they keep making the shapes with the light sneaking through their leaves and suddenly I'm at the corner and turning onto the avenue and ignoring the tourists and the shops and wishing the trees were still there. But then, look at how fat those people are, I bet they're from the Mid-West.

Sense of Self

Melissa performs her morning ritual with a bit of extra care today. This is her day. The day she can become whole. After years of psychiatric counseling and medication, neurological scans, being poked and prodded like a test subject: she's going to get her chance.

She brushes her hair with her right hand, only her right hand. She eats a bowl of cereal and does the dishes, standing up each in the corner of the sink and scouring with a scrubbing pad held tightly in her right fingers.

When Melissa was born, her parents checked her — as all new parents do — finding ten fingers and ten toes. Two baby blue eyes and a few wispy blonde hairs. All the doctors and nurses said how beautiful she was, how she would grow into a gorgeous woman.

And she has, standing statuesque in her nightgown, brushing her teeth, then stretching dental floss, one-handed between her right thumb and index finger. She is clean, and she is ready.

As Melissa grew up, she began experiencing a disconnect from her body. A sense of wrongness that she couldn't quite put her finger on. She tried all the popular options for young woman: not eating at all, or eating then regurgitating. That didn't solve it. She was beautiful, and she knew it. She just felt wrong. Felt as though there was too much of her.

She picks up a bottle of rum, again right-handed, and sets it on the counter, unscrewing the cap and pouring it into a tumbler. She takes a drink, wincing as it burns her throat, and prepares herself mentally.

Her parents noticed something was wrong and sent her to therapists, doctors, and a parade of specialists. She didn't dare be honest with any of them, until college. She had a breakdown and confessed. The doctor told her it was rare, told her it was neurological and treatable. Called it Body Integrity Identity Disorder. She couldn't help but not care: someone else putting a name on it didn't help in the least.

Here and now, she readies her supplies. Using her right hand she ties a rubber-strap tourniquet around her left arm, just above the elbow. She picks up the tumbler of rum again, downing it in one long lug. Her cell phone is on the counter, 911 already typed in. All she has to do is hit send. She reaches for the hacksaw, changes her mind and decides to use the hammer first. She takes a deep breath and knows that today will be hard. But by the end of it, she'll finally be whole.

Oppositional Defiance

Their son screams from his room, where they sent him on the advice of a professional.

"It's painful, but if it's what we have to do…" She trails off with a sigh of resignation.

"I know. I don't like it either." He sits at the kitchen counter, rubbing his hands into his face as though washing it. Heavy bags hang beneath his eyes, bloodshot and weary behind smeared glasses. The counter is cluttered with the remnants of a would-be dinner, interrupted by a tantrum.

"So what do you think?" She asks, looking nervous, "Is it something we did?"

"I honestly don't know. You try to provide freedom, flexibility. Try to keep the kid's life good and happy. Try to give him the things you never had. And then he still ends up like…" Now it's his turn to trail off.

"Ends up like what? Horrible? Broken?" The edge of tears in her voice.

"No. Just… imperfect. My parents had been so strict. They never let me get away with anything. From the time I got home till the time I ate dinner, it was chores and homework and then maybe outside for a few minutes, then dinner and bed. There wasn't any wiggle room. It seems now like there just wasn't time for me to give them any shit."

"I feel like he blames us." Her tears are closer now, looming over the horizon of this conversation.

He extends a hand across the counter, lacing his fingers into hers. She bows her head and breathes out a long, shaky sigh.

"I think he does. But I do too, to be honest. We tried to do our best, and now we just have to hope we can do something different enough to turn this thing around." He knew he was being too optimistic, too casual. 'This Thing' was his son's life. His future.

The screams continued, then eventually faded. They went in to talk with him, to tell him why he'd received the consequences that seemed so harsh to his young mind. They found him asleep, and stood in the doorway, faint memories of watching him sleep 10 years ago. When he was so peaceful, so quiet. So easy.

Triskaidekaphobia

He was late to work. Again.

His boss told him this was going to be his last chance, told him that he'd had too many in the past. It wasn't a great job, but it fulfilled most of the requirements of his odd lifestyle. Working nights, limited interaction with human beings. His last chance to hide safely within the cubicle he had called home for three years.

And now here he was, stuck at a red light, sweat beading on his brow as he white-knuckle grasped the steering wheel, shaking back and forth as though that would change things. Stuck at this corner. Of all corners.

He thought back to being a kid, not afraid of much of anything. He thought of that old saw Frank Herbert coined in Dune: "Fear is the mind killer." How true that was. Once you open those floodgates, let fear in, it dominates and overwhelms you. You don't stand a chance.

He knew that.

When he was young, he had bravely trotted across fallen trees, scampered along sidewalks rife with broken glass and ran confident over the loose rocks of jetties on seaside vacations.

Then puberty struck. Thirteen years into his young life, he found himself clumsy, ungainly, sparse hair and zits sprouting on his face. He was socially useless and physically uncoordinated. He had fallen in gym, on the thirteenth lap of an indoor mile run around a basketball court. His open mouth hit the wooden floor as he called out uselessly. As though saying something could stop a fall. His two front teeth shattered and he wound up in the ER. Everyone had laughed.

Thirteen years old, thirteen laps, and the rest of his miserable life later, he was stuck at the corner of this goddamn street. His job on the line and his heart pounding in his ears. His shirt soaked through.

It was Friday. He couldn't let this happen. The light turned green and he slammed his foot down on the accelerator. Not today. Not this day. Not this Friday.

The Eaten Word

She walks into the antique bookstore, motes of dust falling to the floor in a shaft of sunlight before her. She breathes in the deep, musty smell of books, and breathes out a sigh of relief. She has a very refined palate for someone so compulsive.

Her fingers trace fine lines across the backs of leather-bound volumes. First editions with gold-etched titles and signed frontispieces stood in row after row. The old man at the counter watched her, looking up from his worn copy of To Kill a Mockingbird over scratched half-moon glasses. He watched as she squatted down, wound up on her haunches like a cat ready to spring, extending her hand slowly towards the shelves.

She was in the A's, having just entered the store. Alcott, perhaps. He wondered what she was searching for. Her back to him, he couldn't see that her eyes were closed. She inhaled deeply, running a fingers up and down each spine the way you or I would squeeze and smell fresh fruit at the grocery.

Her long nails left tiny streaks in the dust on the backs of Albee's and Alger's. She etched her hunger into the leather, breathing in the aroma until she could no longer take it. She snatched up a volume and checked the price. $12.99. A small price to pay for satisfaction.

She walked over to the counter and set her purchase in front of the old man. He chuckled and muttered something about crazy historians. He gave her a hand written receipt and wished her happy reading. Watched as she rushed out the door. He shook his head and went back to reading, praying another customer would interrupt him.

She stepped out into the parking lot, paper bag in hand, the urge overtaking her. Unlocking her car, she began to peel back the brown paper containing her prize. Then the plastic and dust-cover that had kept the book safe these many years. She hadn't gotten anything too vintage, but then again the price reflected that. Sometimes rarities go underappreciated.

She opened the book to the title page and saw the signature. A long slow shredding sound as she removed it. John M. Allegro. She savored the feel of the paper in her hands, slippery but textured like finely woven cloth. She opened her mouth and put it on her tongue, feeling 30-year old ink melt into her taste buds.

That would hold her for now. She put the car in gear and drove home, budgeting out her meals from now on. This was a good one, and she planned to make it last.

IV

New York Scenes

The city looms.
In hearts and minds it seems to be
All that ever could.
Beneath its dusky peel
Lies something no one's managed
The depths to plumb.

59th And 5th

  I surface from the stale air of the subway, all my senses inundated. Salesmen hawking movie scripts and trinkets sit passively as the drivers of horse-drawn carriages vie for the attention of passers-by.

  The street is full of traffic, the sounds of horns, squealing breaks and sirens blending with the myriad languages of visiting families. The air is filled with diesel fumes, sweat and the fertile stench of horse excrement.

  I finally allow myself a full breath as I descend the stairs into the park. Leaving the street behind, the man imploring me to rent a bicycle for only five dollars. The light, the heat, and seemingly the city itself. It all fades as I walk down, passing homeless men asleep on the wide stone rails of the stairs.

  I take a seat on a bench and hide behind sunglasses, staring out over the winding, murky body of water in south Central Park.

People pass. Some in conversation, some wearing Jackie-O lunettes and affected looks of disaffection. A man with a face as sober and somber as a judge's walks a tiny smiling Pomeranian. I can't help but smile: break my role of passive observer. The man seems to notice and I'd swear he rolled his eyes behind his dark shades. The subtlest twitch of his neck and shoulders bely his unmerited resentment. It seems to say, "You must not be familiar with local etiquette."

A cluster of sparrows descends on crumbs left behind by a pretzel-chomping child, as a small horde of foreigners ascends the stone above the water. Quiet. Food. Photo ops. We can all find what we need here.

W 48th St.

I stand with Times Square at my back, remembering this block as it was years ago. As a guitar, I think the unique and exciting instruments—the real expense stuff—are rarely worth buying but always worth trying.

Over the past ten years or so, this block has gotten more and more homogenous. It's come to reflect the same sense you get from the billboards in Times Square: that there are, at most, ten companies worth caring about, and they're all owned by two or three bigger companies.

In the past, I could have come here and bounced from store to store, seeing something new and exciting behind each picture window. Now red awnings dominate my view. Sam Ash—hometown chain turned corporate giant—has bought out the competition and replaces each storefront with a different department of their mega-store.

The lone holdout is Rudy's, a high-priced and somewhat snobby shop known for handcrafted instruments and starting the career of legendary luthier John Suhr.

Now even they've joined the homogeneity act. All the unique gear sits unplayed in the front window, the racks stocked with the same high-priced but boring items one would see behind the counter of any guitar shop in America.

The bass room boasts some impressive, $10k+ gear, but the salesman is busily whining about an unsatisfactory gig to a man who's more hanging out than shopping. They seem to relish the bond of the tortured musician, complaining and name-dropping at the same time.

I give up and go downstairs, trying to make bluegrass riffs work on an oud, a traditional Middle Eastern instrument vaguely resembling a guitar or lute. The salesman down here gives me the stink-eye for doing so, so I put it back and go outside, wandering and staring blankly at the windows of

Sam Ash's various departments.

Music Row, as goofy as it sounds, used to mean something. It reflected a proud history of innovation and manufacturing. Craftsmanship. Now it's a brand.

I sigh and shake my head, walking back to 7th Avenue past rows of long-haired kids in the black uniform of Sam Ash sales. They sit in clouds of smoke on their break, squatting on stoops like hobos on commission.

Port Authority

It seems strange that this place should be called a "terminal," as it is no one's final destination. People flood into and out of here, blood cells in the beating heart of an urban giant. Some arrive with luggage or an instrument case, dreams of greatness and opportunities in their head. For others, this is their escape hatch. See them run in from the street, backpacks and handbags bouncing as they rush towards the ticket booth.

They've tried to get people to stay, or at least slow down, adding shops and restaurants to give the great heart the vibe of a suburban mall. Most of them end up being pit-stops: places to fuel up in the midst of a journey elsewhere.

Sitting here fifteen minutes, I must have seen a thousand people. No one's curious about me. No one's even looked — Not even when I caught a whiff of over-applied cologne and sneezed loudly, echoing off the brick walls and terra cotta floor.

One would think a large man sitting cross-legged on the floor of a public space, scratching words into a notebook would attract more attention. But these people aren't really here. They're just passing through. They have their final destinations on their mind, whereas I'm solely here. Stopped in the space between home and away. Sitting nowhere, watching people go everywhere.

Every now and then I look up, seeing new families and individuals go up and down the escalators. A man stops for a croissant, leather bag slung over his shoulder, before disappearing into the masses. A teenage girl from out of town hugs herself against the air conditioning and the leers of strange city men. A mother clutches her two sons' hands in hers, refusing to let go despite their protests.

This isn't somewhere you want to lose someone. This is a frontier, a border town. A crack between tiles in the great mosaic of American society. Fall in, and there might be no getting out.

I put my sunglasses on and get ready to head for the door. I know I'll forget this feeling—this fear—soon enough. I stand up and join the stream.

7 Train, 4:39 PM.

I'd wager there are at least 6 different languages being spoken in this train car, and it's only half full. The 7 is the gateway to some of Queens' more exotic areas, most notably Flushing: a Sino-Korean annex which surrounds the American shrine that is Citi-Field. Home of the Mets in the midst of a quickly spreading spot of Asia.

People board the train at each stop, most alone and affecting a thousand yard stare. Some in a sensory isolation thanks to dark glasses and blaring headphones.

Underwater now, we pass from Manhattan to Queens, a family coaching a young boy to pinch his nose and blow out. His ears pop underneath the plastic wings of a Thor movie helmet.

We climb out of darkness and Long Island City comes into view. Industrial buildings squat and brood around the feet of new swanky riverside apartments. A couple, huddled close with fingers twined around the same rail, lets out a large laugh. The public evidence of some private joke.

The train banks hard to the left and I stand, my seat taken by a small Hispanic woman before I realize I got up two stops too early. A few minutes later I'm exiting the train at Queensboro Plaza to transfer to the N, out in the hot summer air once again.

The N is too crowded, so I decide to hoof it. I pass more rusty, graffiti'd industrial buildings. One bears a shockingly good rendition of Conan the Barbarian: Frazetta lovingly reproduced in rattle-can paint. I pass into more residential districts, relishing the smell of a woman watering her lawn on this hot afternoon.

Before too long, I'm home, safe in the air conditioning and myself again. No longer anonymous, I reflect on the experience of travel in the City. Being one out of too many to count. There aren't any conclusions to come to.

Instead of pondering, I run the shower and wash the grime and sweat from my hair, feeling safe and sound in a space that is, for the moment, just mine. An island in a sea of common areas.

G Train, 10:48 PM

I'm staring at the floor as a podcast blares talk lamenting the existence of lobbyists into my ears. The floor is mottled, melted flecks of red, white and blue plastic in a field of black. I'm idly wondering if that American-flag theme was deliberate, some post-9/11 nod to the country we all supported when this new-ish train was commissioned. Things are a bit different now.

I've spent the night down in Brooklyn, playing Skeeball and drinking beer with a friend from way back. I had a ton of fun, and capped off the evening with the drunken purchase of vegan faux-chicken nuggets and fries. Only in a city like this can you purchase fake chicken made from tofu at 10:30 at night, deep fried, battered and served in plastic basket lined with greasy paper.

The ethics of the city perplex me. It is at once a shrine to decadence, and a paragon of health. Options for both exist around every corner: fried chicken restaurants put french fries on sandwiches, hamburgers are served not on buns but on bisected donuts. At the same time, charities collect on every corner, people buy anything with the word "organic" on it, and gyms and smoothie shops dominate the economic landscape.

Walking through a series of oxymoron pairs. Each one more baffling than the next.

The train grinds to a halt and I hop off to transfer. As I get on the next one, I'm standing and watching stops go by, as usual wondering what it all means. Perhaps it's just like the floor.

Disparate elements held together by an unnameable black goo. A poster reads "Born in the Phillipines, proud American, valuable part of the community," with a friendly Asian woman's face smiling out from it. Maybe that's the point. New York as microcosm. Got a viewpoint or a lifestyle? We've got a place for it, here in the city that makes no sense.

I surface and walk past a driving school, a yoga studio, and a Dunkin Donuts. Opportunities for good and for bad. The disparate elements floating in black goo. Culture.

Or maybe just an ugly set of floor tiles.

Cafe, Wednesday, 1:23 PM

I'm sitting at a table near the bathroom, the only unoccupied spot. Studious folks with laptops and pained expressions on their face take up most tables. One, however, is now filled with high school students, reveling in their break.

Before the other couple joined them, the louder of the two sets were seated across from each other, at one point lying on their sides and loudly conversing underneath the table. The only item proving their patronage of this establishment is a sole half-full cup of Mountain Dew. They argue over something not worth listening to, but my attention is piqued when I hear the girl yell, "You're so immature, dog. I feel like the only mature one over here! What the fuck?"

I'd estimate their age at around 14. Maybe a little older, but not much, judging by the peach-fuzz bordering on pedophile mustache sported by the male facing me. They're a lump of wriggling PDAs and loud obscene arguments, each spoken with the lilting tones of uncertainty that I've come to associate with modern speech. The slow death of the declarative. Every statement a question, just as each movement is a tried-on affectation. Finding oneself by the process of elimination. I'll not be waxing nostalgic about teenage years anytime soon.

I do wonder though, how these kids, despite their brash and interrupting social style, have gotten this far without any hint of self-consciousness. Perhaps its just on a different level, or perhaps this just indicates that what they are self-conscious of is being embarrassed, acting self-conscious.

That'd be interesting.

Their conversation lulls as the couples collapse onto one another, casual hand holding becoming near-choke embraces. His forearm across her neck, elbow resting on her shoulder as she leans backwards into him. This is proof. This is advertising. This says: we've discovered the other sex. We're not quite sure what it's for yet, but we will hold onto it with all we've got. And we will make enough noise to keep you at bay while we figure it out, thank you very much.

I keep the brim of my hat low, and snap their picture. This exercise is making me creepier, but hey: at least I'm quiet about it.

Argument, 1:32 AM

Candidness is an unfortunate side-effect of this type of endeavor. I sit on a futon, which was the subject of some debate upon moving in, eyes stinging and cold, hands cramping from clenching and unclenching. Normally I would couch this in metaphor. Bring in a character, perhaps an addict or a struggling artist who was recently bitten by a werewolf. Try to make it clever. And witty. There's been very little clever or witty about my behavior tonight.

I don't really remember what happened. I remember biological sensations: heartbeat rushing, the sound of my own voice echoing sarcastic questions off the bedroom ceiling. Feelings of shame and self-loathing dominate my current emotional landscape.

The argument, as most are, was essentially about communication. About the problems two people face when forced to—for lack of a better term—face each other. Really face each other. Stand up and be yourself. It's harder than it looks. But when you live with someone, are forced to share your life with them, it becomes an inevitability. All those stolen solo moments go out the window, for better and for worse. Mostly, if you're lucky as I am, for better. Still, this tests the relationship, for obvious reasons. But it also tests your relationship to yourself.

Reflected in the mirror of someone you love, someone who's opinion you truly care about, are you going to like what you see? And, regardless of whether you do or don't, can you truly feel represented? Feel as if they have a good grasp on you.

You almost hope they see the same thing you do. But then you realize, when you're halfway down a dark and windy conversational road, that there are things in there that you see that you don't like. Everyone's got buttons, and the craziest thing is that some twisted part of ourselves needs them to be pushed. If the other person isn't actually pushing them, we scan that sentence—analyze the inflection, even — to find something that pushes it. We invent offenses, giving us license to react in the manner to which we're accustomed.

I use the impersonal "you" in that previous paragraph, but frankly, each of those "you"s and "We"s was really a big fat I. I can't get around it, being human and all. The general rules for human life, as per this writer, are essentially just the rules this writer follows.

Aside: I just caught myself typing "the rules the universe follows" and then realized that that's entirely my interpretation.

To return to the issue at hand: communication. The difficulty of seeing yourself in other's reactions to the ugly bits you've got but pretend you don't most of the time. I think the actual word for that kind of seeing is "intimacy," although I'd have to check a dictionary. Letting down the guard, being honest and open. Being ugly in front of someone you find so beautiful.

It seems inevitable. But it's still an awful fucking feeling.

Heatwave.

   Every building radiates waves of heat, each brick a miniature sun. The wind picks up and suddenly the kiln of the city is transformed into a convection oven, making me squint against air that feels like it would turn my eyes to raisins if given access. This is summer in the city.

   I awake, dry-nosed and coughing, dehydrated from another night's sleep in the required air conditioning. Chugging pints of water all day will only do so much. Between the extreme heat outside and the dry cold of the indoors, I'm bound to lose gallons. As I walk down the sidewalk, I begin to wonder if your shoes are feeling sticky. If the rubber's melting or if I could really crack an egg and watch the gelatinous white go cloudy, eventually turning opaque and crackling on the concrete surface. The heat radiates in visible waves, the optical illusions of oases in the middle of a crowded street.

   Everywhere I turn there are people, sweating

and cursing under their breaths. Overweight men still get up and put on their suits, ties and shirt-collars soaked through with sweat. Women wear skimpy clothes and roll their eyes at anyone who looks at their midriffs or barely covered cleavage. Everyone is angry. They want respite. They need reprieve. There's nowhere to hide but indoors. As I pass the open doorways of shops and restaurants, the cold air of their air-conditioning — made freezing in contrast — licks at my ankles, tempting me to enter. But if I do, I soon become cold. The meager scraps of gym shorts and t-shirts I don to give myself breathing room can't handle the constant blast of refrigerated air. And besides, it only makes it worse when I step outside. Back out into that shining heat. Waves of air assaulting my exposed skin, the sun tries to blind me.

The whole neighborhood has taken on an awful golden color. Normally gray tiles of sidewalk seem to reflect pure light, glowing yellow with accumulated heat. Bricks shine a bright angry red as the windows they surround are turned into blinding mirrors.

All these buildings, all these people, absorbing the sun's rays and clinging to them. The only thing to do is hide indoors, out of the sun. Praying that the energy doesn't penetrate the bricks deep enough to get me — deep enough to turn my sanctuary, my home, into an oven itself.

The interesting thing is: I've been to hotter places. I've stood in the Australian desert. I've been in the American southwest and grew up in North

Carolina, where 100+ degree-days with 100% humidity weren't uncommon. But there's nothing quite like this. And it comes back to the bricks, which I've mentioned over and over.

Every brick is like a shooting star, flying in formation, allowing our world to cohere and thestructures they form to stay composed. But the energy radiating off of so much stone, so much clay, so many non-reflective surfaces. The sheer mass of the city absorbing the sun's limitless power and holding onto it, regurgitating it slowly, throughout the day and the night. Eventually the city itself becomes a greater threat than the sun. Especially when you add the people.

Heat. Bricks. People. Sweat. Discomfort. Anger.

Summer in the city.

Respite

The cool came before the rain, not afterwards, as it so often does. The morning was cloudy, the skies breaking in the mid-afternoon. Droplets fell in bursts, chilling the skin and summoning umbrella salesmen to their posts. They stood on corners, duffle bags stuffed with portable protection from the elements, capitalizing on the kindness of nature as they cried pitches at passersby.

Now it's night, and a soft breeze make the hairs on the back of my neck stand up, a delicious physical reaction to such a welcome change. The city smells of wet asphalt and plants, as though they themselves are sighing with relief.

The sky is a smooth, grey-green dome of light pollution, brightening to the west, where Manhattan stands alight behind the darkened church next door. The sound of air conditioners continues. They emit their urban cricket drone as they cool the interiors of large apartment buildings, ghosts of hundred-plus degree-days still haunting the brick walls.

It seems quieter than normal. As if the whole city has rolled over and lapsed into a deep and much needed sleep. Just as I'm contemplating the stillness, a man exits a house and pulls a car into the driveway, shutting the red-painted iron gate behind him while eyeing me suspiciously. I make no attempt to explain my presence. I simply inhale, look up at the sky once more, and exhale the night air back into itself. I worry that I've spoiled it with the heat of my lungs and the movement of my body in the stillness.

The street still shines black with rain, and large drops are visible on the cars. The humidity keeps them there, jewels encrusting the black paint jobs of Town Cars and vans. In each, the yellow glow of the humming streetlight above glistens: still reflections of the quiet street, distorted into tiny round stars.

There's no one out. No one walking. No rushing or hurrying or stress. I stand still for five minutes and not a single car drives down our block.

It's beautiful.

Metropolitan Avenue, Brooklyn

I'm in Williamsburg, Brooklyn — the ironically beating heart of hipsterdom — because an old friend asked me to help him move a mattress. After 20 minutes of negotiating the monstrous sponge of Tempur™ material down winding stairs, we had a couple of beers and went our separate ways. He to the van in which his bed now resides, and I underground.

The G-train runs sparsely, but there's entertainment to be had. A banjo player has strapped a tambourine to one foot and kicks a wooden box turned bass drum with the other. The jury-rigged one man bands provides a manic soundtrack to the comings and goings of the young and terminally-cool residents of the neighborhood. They pass me by without a glass in my shorts and T-shirt. They wear tight-fitting, trendy clothing, bright colors mixed equally with dingy, unwashed whites.

One man attracts my attention. He squats on his haunches, back against the stained tile of subway station wall. His sweat-matted hair parts in the middle, dark red curls spilling down weather side of his head. Blue eyes glare like the headlights of oncoming traffic, challenging the world. Open on his lap is a notebook of unlined paper. Covered in crude sketches, faces marked out with a few shaky lines.

His eyes return to the paper, then to a tanned, muscular man with a sleeveless shirt on. The oblivious model has a strong jaw, an aquiline nose and a pompadour of thick, blue-black hair.

The drawing has a clumsy hooked schnozz and hair like a drawn Brillo pad, swirled circles of pen representing the individual strands. Still the artist keeps working, staring from under furrowed brows at is subject over the rims of plastic, tinted glasses.

By this point I feel I've dropped out of the scene, into some safe position of observer. I keep my back firmly pressed to the fourth wall.

But then the squatting artist turns his furtive, gloomy gaze on me. I stare at nothing in particular and suppress a chuckle. Imagining I'm posing for my portrait. I think to him, loudly:

"You and I, my creepy friend, we are not so different. Except, of course, no one knows when I'm taking their picture."

The train arrives and I'm faintly disappointed as he closes the notebook and places it in a large canvas tote bag. He stands, revealing stained gray jeans and a V-neck shirt, exposing more of his chest than an evening gown would. He runs fingers through the greasy curls of his hair, preening in front of his reflection in the train window.

I stand across from where he sits for two stops. I feign interest in my phone and surreptitiously snap a picture of him, feeling a certain kinship. Sure, he seems more out in the open, perhaps more than a little pretentious, but ultimately all he was doing was collecting faces.

And I took his picture, observed his behavior. I cataloged and caricatured him in one fell swoop. The reason the pen is mightier than the sword is as follows: with a sword, you can execute. With a pen, you pass judgment. You set a moment in writing, imprisoning the character, holding him fast and fixed despite variation in behavior over the passage of time.

In many ways, a story is like a portrait, scrawled in a notebook on a subway track. An unflattering, unrealistic memory, recorded for the artist. Whether for practice or simply for the joy of making someone else your own.

Of course, some are better than others.

New York: An Essay.

The City.

Why do people come here? Choose to live in discomfort, cramped spaces and surrounded by unpleasant, unfriendly strangers? A hundred years ago, they would have flocked to ports for work and the ready availability of goods. Manufacturing, shipping and receiving… The holy trinity of trade.

So what brings them here now, when the 'Net and mail order business allow the right kind of business to make just as much money in rural Wisconsin as this megapolis. The answer is relatively easy. We are gulls, flocking to great heaps our of nations greatest export: Bullshit.

It comes in by the metaphorical barge-full, with us converging on these bright spots on an otherwise dull map to lap it up. We bring it with us, we create it here, and almost above all else: we participate in it here.

The "art" scene is a vibrant pastiche of scammers. They exploit their shamelessness, lazily creating diversions for all of us. Minimal effort, maximum noise. Most of it is deritive, but even when it isn't, one man's "experimental" is the everyman's bullshit, if you look close enough. The worst part, of course, is that we are complicit. We allow and indeed encourage the wool to be pulled over our eyes.

One could easily think that the key to success in the creative arts in this place is pure, unbridled confidence. Whether innate or merited, realistic or fictional, confidence keeps the wheels turning. Belief in the importance of one's ideas… Enough to convince financiers and the audience itself, that is true power. And this is the only environment wherein that power can really be exercised.

Of course, there are oases in this desert of pompous noise. There must be. Not because it's true that this place provokes or promotes creativity, but because the odds support it. Wade through enough garbage, you're bound to find something worthwhile. And there's an awful lot of garbage here.

    Downer.

    But that means there should be more good stuff than somewhere else?

    Upper?

9/11/11

Everywhere today we are told not to forget. As though we could. Living in the shadow of the Manhattan skyline, I paused and thought today while on a rooftop garage. The Empire State building peered at me from across the river, and I thought to myself: "That skyline is short two buildings."

I was a senior in high school when the whispers began. A warm, and unreasonably sunny Tuesday morning. People said something about a plane hitting the World Trade Center, and everyone, of course, assumed it was an accident. Until the second plane hit.

Then there was fear, confusion. A gaggle of privileged young things attempting to reach their parents who worked in the city. Tears and fears. Huddled groups, drawing each other close as though bodily warmth would amount to safety and sanity.

This was the effect it had on teenagers. Near-adults.

Now, I sit, and I think of those who were children. The ones who were so young, who never got to taste the life of 1980's and 1990's security. Who perhaps never got to feel safe. They might have been confused at the time, but a milestone had been reached. We had been attacked, on our home soil.

Then there are the children born after. Born into a whirling world of uncertainty, raised in the shadow of a dark event on a sunny day. Raised with no knowledge of peace. No sense of what used to be right and decent.

The consequences have been enormous. Ten years of warfare, a burgeoning military, the collapse of economy and the rise of a clumsy modern empire. And the footage, burned into all of our heads. Planes silently gliding into steel structures as the amateur videographers gasp.

I never had a strong sense of what it was to be American, and still don't. We lack an identity, as a young and complex nation. People use 9/11 to galvanize, to unite. With Us or Against Us. Simple divisions and definitions. Someone on the radio today actually said "Never forgotten, and never forgiven."

What an awful attitude.

Is that what we are to be, a reactionary nation of the vengeful? The bitter mass of anger that wanted so desperately to lash out at our attackers, to destroy an enemy we couldn't find?

I hope not.

Today I don't just remember buildings falling, or the wars that ensued, or even the fact that a group of people found this country (or at least some of its qualities) so repugnant that they would do such a thing.

I remember the lives changed. The lives ended. And the lives that never had a chance to relax in the hazy, ill-remembered days before the event itself.

We've all lost something, whether it's a person, a sense of security, or even just the blessed ignorance of being attacked.

That is what we should remember. That is what I felt today, as I stood looking through haze and a mist of rain at the iconic silhouette of Manhattan. I felt loss, and for a moment, I felt as though I was lost.

I hope we can find our way back to peace and happiness. I hope that we can forgive. Not necessarily the individuals involved, for they are beyond forgiveness, but certainly forgiving the world for being a hostile place. Forgiving society for being an ugly thing at times. And forgiving ourselves for our reactions, for our violence rooted in fear. Telling us never to forget seems to me to get in the way of that. Today I remember. Tomorrow I'll live my life. But each time I see the skyline of the city, I'll still think: two are missing. Two are lost.

V

Interlude: 2 Tales of Ol' Kentucky

If a gun were held to his head
Even stalwart Uncle Remus
Would be forced to admit
That he too had certain irregularities.

The Beaver and His Dam.

Now, Ol' Kentucky, it ain't like Kentucky. It exists in the hazy never in between moments. An age ago, when things were "better than they are now, and you better goddamn believe it now get me my dinner." It's a hallowed place, always spoken of with respect and a tear of wist just teasing at the corner of a cloudy eye.

It was home to all manner of animals. But Ol' Man Beaver was the grumpiest.

Ol' Man Beaver built up that dam all summer, only to have it taken away in a flood.

He wept over the shattered remains of his once great home. His castle. And he dreamed sweet silent dreams of concrete at night. Rebar, drywall. These were the materials he needed. Anything to keep the water out. His coat grew shaggy, his tail flopped from disuse. He didn't do anything but sleep in a nest made of sticks, pining for a concrete dam.

So one morning he went on down to Home

Depot. To get himself supplies. "Bring me spackle! Bring me bucket of cements!" he cried into the crowd of orange-apron wearing elderly, disregarding grammar and Grandma alike. The employees tried to be accommodating, but they had a hard time understanding him, because of his teeth. He hadn't chewed wood in some time, and as such he had developed a considerable lisp.

His scaly tail pounded the concrete floor as he gesticulated wildly at a pile of aluminum siding. The employees began to back away, afraid. But one brave young man, predictably named Timmy Helpful, decided he could be of service. Timmy stepped forward, chest puffed out like a cartoon robin, head thrown back. His limp chin jutted into the fluorescence of warehouse shopping as he proclaimed: "Mr. Beaver? I believe I can be of some assistance."

Old Man Beaver turned around and peered at young Tim from beneath suspicious eyebrows, lips curled back to unveil yellow teeth. He spoke in broken, halting phrases: "Spackle! Need to patch! The dam! Burst! Life's work! Ruined!" The last word came out "ROOOOOOONT." He looked like a madman. Except a beaver.

Timmy Helpful stopped and thought a moment, considering the Beaver's predicament. He decided he knew what to do. Right then and there. He stretched his hand out, inviting Old Man Beaver's scaly paw, and led him to the lumber yard. Here all manner of wood awaited, from weather-treated pine to the flexing, sawdust and glue sheets of ply used in treehouse construction by less than loving parents.

Timmy said to the Beaver, he said: "Mr. Beaver, I know you've had a rough time of it lately. That flood took your home away from you. And that's a sadness I can't rightly understand. But I don't think your salvation lies in spackle any more than comfort comes from stuffing a beehive down your shorts," here he paused to spit, red-black tobacco stains spreading on the pavement, "I think what you need is some quality wood."

Old Man Beaver's eyes lit up, a whole forest of trees, all taken care of and bundled into easy dimensions for him lay behind the Home Depot. He looked up at Tim's stupidly shining face above his orange apron and whispered a word of thanks, a tear of joy crusting up the corner of his beady beaver eye.

Then he began to chew. And chew. And move, rearrange, perhaps stretch, and then chew some more. A crowd looked on, and hours went by. Every once in a while a nice man from the plywood factory arrived in a truck to sweep up sawdust. Nothing goes to waste in Ol' Kentucky. Especially not sawdust. Soon, the beaver had constructed a dam so mighty, water-sealed and Thompson-protected, that no flood could wash it away. Old Man Beaver stood atop it and shook his head, thumped his tail against the damp exterior of the solid pine and ash, and flashed a smile of perfect, pearly white teeth. He was reborn, animal and man combined. The essence of the country life he longed to live.

No longer would he be haunted by cement walls, or thoughts of that accursed substance known as spackle. He could live in purity. A house built from wood and spit and sweat, as was his way.

It should be noted, of course, the dam was in the parking lot of Home Depot. And Old Man Beaver, being a beaver, he didn't have any money. Tim was fired on the spot, and had to move into that dam with the beaver. Couldn't pay his rent, t'weren't any other options.

They brought it out to the river on the back of Pa Helpful's truck. Placed it atop some rocks, where water could spill down underneath it . And there they lived, in the indiscriminate afternoons of Ol' Kentucky, partners. But never, and Ol' Man Beaver would chew me off at the knees if I didn't include this, never lovers.

There's somethings even a beaver won't do, no matter how desperate things get.

Escaping To Home: Skinflap's New Citizen

Ol' Kentucky, it bears belaboring, is not to be confused with regular Kentucky. It is not a land of seersucker suits and wispy mustached chicken salesmen. It's a land that exists in the misty maybes of nostalgia, the wink of an old woman serving you homemade pie. Her nametag says "Grandma." It was always hot in Ol' Kentucky, and that was part of the problem.

No one was quite sure how an old polar bear came to live on the outskirts of Skinflap. The town itself was sure he'd been part of a circus, left when he got too old and his fur too mottled with dry leaves and ticks to maintain. The circus would want a sparkling white bear, if they were to bother dragging his 2-ton carcass around. They imagined a cruel ringmaster, with a big city accent and rings on his pinkies as he twirled a waxed mustache, cackling with glee as the animal was forced out of its trailer.

They were wrong. Dead wrong. But then, the people of Skinflap weren't known for their mental skills. The town itself was founded around a sharp rock, where the founder himself had fallen. Douglas Thackeray Westmoreland had been out for a walk, pioneering about in the woods some two hundred eighty years ago, when he slipped and cut his leg, badly. The wound was so egregious, it required seventeen bottles of corn liquor for him to stop screaming. Left on the prong of that sharp rock was rag of hairy dermis, pale and dripping in the summer breeze. With Westmoreland in no shape to travel, he simply founded a town. A town born of a mistake, and born to make more, to be sure.

Two hundred sixty seven years later, reports of a Sasquatch or similarly ridiculous creature began to circulate amongst the thirty seven people who still called Skinflap home. A great white beast, they would say, emerged from the underbrush, groaning and roaring. Making a general racket that they found disturbed the quiet life they'd relished all these years. Eventually a meeting was called, the ceremonial stick—adorned with Christmas bells and fake feathers—passed amongst the sweating elders gathered in the town square. They elected a single man to do the job. Douglas Thackeray Westmoreland XI would go and find out.

It is important to note that the Westmoreland's refused, for the most part, to breed outside their own. They would marry cousins or make alliances with other families — Lending a royal air to their particular breed of stupidity. Douglas the eleventh (or Dougie L, as he was known) was no exception to this rule of inbreeding and idiocy. He sported a bright red wig that sat atop his head, as illfitting as a bathmat on a rocketship. His head was long and thin, his eyes bloodshot, and his skin nearly translucently pale. He looked, for all intents and purposes, like a twisted inbred mountain freak. Because he was.

Dougie L mounted up the next day, riding out of town astride a reasonably priced Donkey named Christopher. Christopher's hooves clip-clopped along the ruts of the dirt road until the forest lay ahead of them. Suddenly there was a great roar and racket, nearby trees shedding acorns like dandruff. Dougie L mastered up his courage and spoke:

"Hey! ... Hey now! Let's.. not be doing that, then." A beat of silence, and then the reply, a voice like stones grinding against one another.

"I won't do any tricks."

"..."

"I won't fetch or roll over or play dead. I don't care how good your treats are."

"Are you a giant dog?"

A violent roar, a sound of anger, and then the elongated, pale yellow snout broke the tree line.

"I AM NOT A DOG."

Dougie L shook with fear. His bladder and buttocks quaking, he readied his next question. "Okay… That's fine. In fact, that's good! We have enough dogs in this town. They breed like rabbits, except the fur isn't as fine and people frown when you hunt them." The last bit was true, as was demonstrated by several legal cases the preceding year. Much frowning-upon was done in Skinflap, Ol' Kentucky.

"Good. Now that we have an understanding, I will reveal myself to you. If you promise not to run away. If you run away, I'll have to chase you."

"Alright," Dougie trembled, his voice quavering like a soprano on a Magic Fingers™ bed. "Here I come"

From the forest there emerged a glorious sight, a beautiful polar bear, standing on his hind legs. His belly was the soft white of driven snow, his nose and eyes black as onyx. Their obvious carnivorous design belying a tender nervousness. "You… you didn't run! Thank you, thank you sir!"

"Of course." Dougie exhaled for the first time in minutes, trying to sound casual. "Why would I run from one of God's most noble creatures."

"Most people do."

"If I might ask, Mr. Bear… Do you have a name?"

"My name is Dennis Turlington."

"Oh." Dougie supposed he was shocked. He had assumed bears would have magical, spiritual names. Like Amos or Glandril. "My name is Douglas. Douglas Thackery Westmoreland XI. It's nice to meet you. Do you mind if I ask how you came to the edge of our town?"

The bear sighed, deep breath rattling like the sound of an approaching steam train. "It is a sad tale. I was bought, kidnapped from my family and my home. Everything I know. The snow, the summer midnight sun. As a baby I was taken and shipped to a man, a private collector over yonder ridge. He meant to keep me as a pet. He taught me to walk on a leash, to fetch, to roll over and allow him to degrade me with his belly-scratches. I broke free some months ago and have wandered, searching for water and the sweet flesh of fish. Have you got any fish?" Dennis' eyes brightened at the idea of a nice, scaly, oily fish wriggling as he bit it in half.

"Er... Not on me."

"Oh. Well. Okay."

Dougie had an idea! The exclamation point is there to convey the rarity of this occurrence. "What if... you were to live in the river here in Skinflap? It's about two miles up the hill, away from the town and people, plenty of brook trout and flappers" — a 'rare' species of minnow found only in this area — "for you to eat! It'd be perfect!"

A tear crept into the corner of the bear's great bead of an eye, and he fell forward onto all four paws, head bowed. "Your kindness... it is remarkable in a human. Thank you, Douglas. Thank you, so much."

The bear moved into a shack upstream of Old Man Beaver's great plywood dam, wiling away the rest of his days and covering his shameful past by never discussing it. The people of Skinflap simply let him be, every once in a while asking him to do things only he could do. Take down a tree in one swipe or reach something off a shelf so high they wondered why they'd built it in the first place.

Dennis Turlington, the polar bear, lived the of his life in that town, growing fat from fish and limited amounts of frolicking. He passed into local legend, the civilized beast of the wild woods, and slowly faded into the patchwork quilt of lies and nonsense that people call "history" in Ol' Kentucky.

VI

Reasons to Fear Nature: An Aborted Comedic Gimmick.

The words so oft repeated.
They ought to have been laid in stone long ago.
Simply put:
They can't all be winners.

June 2nd, 2009: The Day I Learned of the Coconut Crab

Allow me to set the scene. A brief image search of the Internet for the "coconut crab" will net you a variety of pictures of enormous crustaceans the color of splotchy mud, sprawled out across garbage cans and wandering through fields. They scavenge and clatter, looking for lost food and dead animals to feast upon.

There are a large variety of reasons why such a creature should frighten you. For one, crabs are largely a sea-based demographic. They don't come up and fuck with our stuff. The coconut crab, which lives largely on the islands of the South Pacific, lives most of its life on land, can grown to be 30 pounds, and wants your garbage. In addition to wanting your garbage, it is called the coconut crab not because of any real resemblance to that most majestic of fruits– The only one I know of to triple up as drink ingredient, drink container, and makeshift bra-cup– but because its claws are capable of cracking into one so that the crab might sup upon the milky white goodness within. I want you all to think about something. When's the last time you opened a coconut without difficulty? Your answer was either "Never" or a God damned lie.

What I find worse, if there is something worse than something that looks like it ought to clamp on your head and suck your brain out eating your garbage, is the fact that so-called "scientists" working for the good of so-called "humanity" are fascinated by the thing! Leave it alone! Who cares if it can smell on land or underwater? While admittedly that would be quite a trick if a person did it, this thing is clearly just going to use it to gain the odor-advantage regardless of whatever arena our final battle with it takes place in.

So, long story short. It's a 30 pound, garbage-lustful, shell-less hermit crab and it is coming to destroy us all.

Nuke the coconut crabs, save the world.

The Botfly

What's that? Yes, I said a fly. It's a particularly ugly one, too. Though I'm not sure if the adult is what we ought to be worried about.

If one looks up the adult specimen, he or she will be treated to a view of something that looks slightly uglier than a housefly. Not particularly spectacular, but still slightly skin-crawl-inducing, with its cilia and compound eyes.

Can compound eyes be shifty? If so, I feel the botfly has mastered that skill.

However, it is the reproductive habits of the botfly and the activities of its larva that truly make this insect an abomination. Ordinarily, insects lay eggs in large sacs or clutches, and they hatch peacefully in corners above barn doors or while hanging on the backs of leaves in the summer sun. But no, that simply doesn't satisfy the perverse demands of the botfly, whose particular kink makes the entire cast of Blue Velvet look like an old neutered married couple.

The adult female botfly does not lay its eggs in a clutch or charming satchel, nor does it even have the politeness to lay them in the body of a dead animal like a regular carrion fly. Instead, it catches a mosquito and lays them on its back. Then the mosquito is released and allowed to go about its business. When the skeeter bites something, the eggs are activated by the body heat, hatch, and tiny larvae drop off the mosquito and onto the host, where they burrow into hair follicles and attach themselves using *deep breath* two anal hooks.

At this point, you or the animal in question are/is alive, well, and has a maggot holding onto the inside of your skin by its anus. I know, it's like a goddamn death metal song, but worse. At this point the larva feasts on the host, growing until it eventually erupts from a now infected wound, and I guess gets on with its lifecycle, which revolves around shitting eggs on other bugs and getting its children to burrow into your flesh.

In this world where surrogate mothers are accepted or revered, the botfly has found a way to twist that. It forces not only the eventual host, but also the mosquito to act as a gestational playground for its sickening maggot offspring, and I would argue that this is tantamount to a complex, interspecies game of rape-tag. I would throw up, but I used it all up writing the first three paragraphs.

To sum up, presuming that the worst thing created by humans hovers somewhere between Japanese octopus pornography and nuclear warfare, the botfly outdoes us all, continuing its species in a fashion that would make Caligula blush and Larry Flynt… well, probably sit there, fart loudly, giggle and forget what he was supposed to be outraged about. But if his cognitive faculties were intact and not rotten by his medical conditions and his penchant for drink, boy howdy would he be upset.

The only possible advice I can give you is the following. It may not be clever, or classy, or even reasonable, but please, please, if you value your lives and sanity: stay the hell out of nature.

VII

Life, Death and Disconnection: An Internet Serial

The deep-seated fears of the thinking man
Family and the consequences.
The toll of availability
The mourning of regrets.
Will I make a man, or a monster?
The question echoes, thankfully
Unanswered for now.

Hospital. 11:13AM. August. Years Ago.

The husband stood nervously in the hallway, picking at his teeth and studying his fingernails as though the resolution to his anxieties lay crusted beneath the yellowed tips. He had been up all night. His hair was a greasy brush, short and dark and sticking off his head at odd angles. Two light brown eyes peered out from rings of dark and puffy skin. He read the poster on the wall for the hundredth time. Instructions on how to use the special sink below, with two small nozzles for cleaning harmful substances out of the eyes. What the hell could get into your eyes at the hospital?

His wife had gone into labor the previous night, just before bed. She went to the bathroom and returned, saying in a rushed whisper: "I think it's happening." He rolled from the bed to his feet in one clumsy motion, standing there in his pajamas, and froze. He knew they'd packed a bag, prepared, discussed all this. But in that moment he, for the life of him, could barely remember how to walk, speak, or breathe. His nerves were killing him and he wasn't even having the damned thing.

Thing. He supposed he'd have to get used to calling it by a name. It hadn't been intentional, but it was a blessing of a sort. The type of thing a young couple is meant to do. He had a steady job working as a salesman for a local advertising firm. He'd meet with clients, schmooze and dine with them, all in attempts to sell a two-by-two inch square of printing space in the local paper. His wife was the perfect model of a housewife of the time, right down to her pet social justice cause — Native American rights — and her constant boredom.

It'd be any minute now. They'd come out and get him. He didn't want to go. He shoved the tip of one fingernail into the gap between his two front teeth, convinced that a seed was lodged there. He found nothing other than the glistening spit-covered tip of his finger, and the coppery salt twang of blood issuing forth from his gums.

Why couldn't this be over?

The doorway swung open, and a small man in a green uniform came out. He wore pants and a shirt, covered with a paper gown, topped off with a small cap of the same material. The husband thought he looked like the world's shittiest Christmas gift, but stood anyways, his eyes turned upwards in what he hoped was a benign hopeful gesture and not a betrayal of his internal discomfort.

"A boy. Come in. Meet your son."

At that, the husband found he could breathe again. Suddenly a weight lifted off his chest and the muscles moved slowly and confidently. A smile twitched at the corner of his mouth. In his mind's eye, he saw baseball games, bike-riding lessons. Teaching the kid how to throw a punch, just in case. He found himself excited, and hurriedly walked towards the doctor, taking long strides.

They went into the room. His wife lay beneath a paper sheet, drenched with sweat, hair matted to her head. She beamed, her perfect white smile shining down in benevolence on the tiny form lying on her chest. Her eyes were moist and unfocused from the nights effort.

"He's perfect," she said as her husband came to her side. "Just perfect."

The husband cautiously used his finger to pull back the blanket in which the babe was swaddled. A tiny hand flopped forth and found the intruder, grabbing it with a grip-strength that shocked him. He let out a surprised, single laugh, and found himself transfixed. All his anxieties disappeared. He melted into the moment, like ice slowly giving way to spring. His mind was a fog of good wishes and blissful ignorance of what was to come.

"Yes, he is," he agreed. "Yes he is."

Homecoming: Day 1.

They returned early the next morning, still smiling but crumpled from their second night at the hospital. A pile of mail greeted them, drooling out of the slot onto the floor of the entryway. They ignored it, instead both focusing on the tiny bundle of joy in her arms. The father set about building a crib in the spare room, something he'd been putting off for months; while she sat in the kitchen, cooing and tickling as tiny uncomprehending eyes gazed up at her.

At last the crib was built, the padded mattress installed, and a cadre of blankets assembled to support and comfort the child in his new home. The parents stood, arm in arm, each with a hand tenderly perched on the rail and stared down at him. Her head nestled beneath his chin, she softly began to weep. He asked if she was all right. She said she was just so happy. Her face turned up towards his, and her eyes shined as her teeth showed in a glittering grin.

The first night was hard. The child cried every three hours, meeting his needs with the only mode of expression available to him. The mother spent at least twenty minutes in with him each time, and on the third instance, she didn't come back.

There were no more cries.

The new father awoke on his back the next morning, sprawled across the bed. His eyes half opened and he shut his mouth, wiping a cold trickle of spittle from the corner of his mouth. He called his wife's name, but received no answer.

Worrying about postpartum issues and the raging hormones of the recently pregnant, he ran to his new son's new room. There he found her, sitting asleep in a rocking chair she'd dragged in from the back patio. One arm lolled down by her thigh, where it had clearly been outstretched towards the sleeping infant.

The father smiled to himself the hazy smile of relaxation and padded back to bed.

When he awoke again, it was midday. Bright sun shone in through the windows and his head throbbed, though he finally felt rested. He showered and dressed and went into the boy's room to check on his wife. She was still sitting there, motionless, beatific smile plastered to her face. He asked if she'd had breakfast.

"What?" His voice had shocked her from her reverie. Food and concerns of her own body were the furthest from her mind. "No. No, I suppose I haven't."

"You need to eat!" he chided in a harsh but pleasant whisper,

"You've been through a lot too. Besides, if you don't stay healthy, how can you take care of him?"

"I just," she began. She hesitated, her expression doubtful as she took her eyes off the bundle in the crib. "I just don't want to leave. I can't explain it."

"Maybe this is something all mothers go through. Separation. It must be stressful. I can't pretend to understand." The husband played a contrite role: helpful yet emphasizing his ignorance. This was often his way in disputes. He apologized before the argument even started, using misunderstanding as a manipulative tool.

"I suppose." Her eyes drifted back to the crib, her left hand instinctively reaching towards it. "It's as though the world's gone black and white. And he's the only spot of color left in it." Tears streamed silently down her face, her smile never wavering.

The father stepped quietly back into the hallway and went to the kitchen. He got bread and eggs and milk out of the refrigerator. Brewed coffee and plugged in the toaster. And hoped his wife was just going through a phase.

The First Year

His wife had become more and more reclusive. She sat by the crib, gazing at her child over the top of a magazine. The same page facing her for hours and hours. She was thinner now than she had been before pregnancy, save the life giving swelling of her chest. Her face was gaunt and trifold dark rings encircled her eyes. But she was happy.

He would drive to work each day, after exhorting her to get out, take the child for a walk. They hadn't bought that ludicrously expensive designer stroller for nothing, had they? Each time, she would nod. Look through him and mutter, "Sure, sure. That's the plan." After a long day of work, buying and selling, going through increasingly harsh negotiations in uncertain times, he would return home. And find her sitting there. Right where he left her.

She must get up at some point. She hadn't died, so she must be eating. She can't answer the call of the nature from that rocking chair with the ratty woven cushion.

He was hesitant to speak of these things at work. Too embarrassed to ask for advice, he'd answer "Fine" whenever anyone asked how she was doing, and "She's very busy" when anyone asked why they hadn't seen her in months. Summer came and she demanded he move the window-unit air conditioner to the child's room. "For the baby," she implored. He suspected it was true. She cared for that tiny, brainless thing more than for herself.

He had begun to resent the attention his son received. He assumed this was normal, but felt inside him a black pit of bile, growing stronger and threatening to break through. He repressed it as best he could, but it came out in other ways. First he was a half hour late one day, aimlessly driving the side streets and back-routes near his house. Soon he began fixing himself dinner and a tall drink before even going to check on her. By Fall, he had given up.

He would sit for hours himself, hiding behind the newspaper in a blue-upholstered chair in the living room. His feet shifting nervously, one on top of the other, then vice versa. At times the child would cry out, and immediately be answered by her insipid, muttered coos. He could never hear what she said to him. Didn't want to. Not anymore.

Perhaps, he would think after a few belts of gin or scotch, this is just what parenthood is. You take a backseat to your wife's new love. Her tiny, helpless replacement husband. After all, she can only take care of so much at any given time. And face it, pal… You just aren't it anymore.

He knew this must be wrong though. From his own childhood, he remembered both his parents being involved, giving attention in their own misbegotten way. His mother was kind, his father a cold disciplinarian. Regardless of their parenting styles, he still remembered sneaking down to the top of the stairs, watching their stolen moments. They would gaze at each other across a candlelit table, enjoying their private dinner. He would hear his father laugh, a sound he rarely heard when he was underfoot. His mother spoke at length about things other than the gossip he would overhear in the station wagon.

They had a child, but they still had lives. A life. Together.

Where had it gone?

A Letter From The Father: Year 4.

It's amazing how fast disappointment fades into acceptance. How I could be so distraught one day then over time lose hold of that feeling. It slipped from my fingers, like a cliff's edge, and I tumbled into the abyss of routine.

The boy is 4 tomorrow. He started preschool a few months back and of course the reports have been great. Gold stars. All gold stars. Glittering sheets of meaningless grades. How do you grade a 3 year old? It says he follows directions. The only direction is "Play over here with this thing you love." If only life could be that simple for the rest of us.

My wife's been a wreck since he's started. He's only gone for three hours a day, but she still sits in that rickety old chair, elbow propped on the armrest, hand shaking as her crossed legs bounce up and down with nervous energy. She looks like a junkie in withdrawal. I won't lie and say I've tried to help. Serves her right.

Shit. I can't believe I wrote that down. I guess what I mean is that she should have seen him for what he was. A parasite. A curly haired, blue-eyed parasite. Behind the dimpled cheeks and soft, chubby fingers lies something that just wants to use her up. I'm not even sure if he knows it. In fact, I doubt he does. He doesn't pay her any mind. Just goes about his day, learning words and stacking blocks as she follows him fulfilling any need he expresses. Spoiled rotten.

He's innocent, in his way. He's tried to connect to me. Tried to get me to drop the walls I began putting up a week after he came home from the hospital. But I've seen what he did to her. I know not to let him in. I sit and grunt noncommittally when he toddles up to me and pulls down the newspaper. My shield. The chair I picked years ago is now worn, the imprint of my expanding waistline eroded into the fabric, two bare patches from my forearms resting on the sides. It's a damned fine chair.

What started as an escape has simply become

life. What started as hell has become boring. That's what I mean about the abyss of routine. It sucks you in, slowly, reassuring you that things are consistent. That you can adjust to anything. That you don't have to fear change, because there isn't any.

That's what life has become.

He makes everyone happy, you know. My wife lights up when he's in the room. She runs over and kneels down, helping him out of his little jacket after the carpool drops him off. She touches his face, lightly, as though to make sure he's still real. The other mothers all ooh and ah over his blue eyes, his increasing manners and vocabulary. The children gather around, and join in whatever he's doing. It's like he's a conductor, and the world is his orchestra.

You know I actually saw a stranger at the supermarket stop and smile at him, that same stupid dreamy look the wife had that first night? The woman waved. Her wrist was kind of limp, tick-tocking a hand back and forth like a soggy metronome. She looked so goddamned happy.

Why does everyone enjoy my son except me?

They're coming out now. Out into my space. I need to put my shields back up. I'll write more when I get a chance. There's no escape for me right now. Only defense. Hope you're well. Hope we can see each other soon.

Birthday Memories

An image floats into his mind. He's lying on his bed, the padded quilt beneath him. In the black of his closed eyes, he sees. He remembers.

A row of flashbulbs goes off, bright white sugar cubes exploding as one atop the black and blue plastic frame of his mother's camera. He's at the head of the table, staring out at rows of smiling faces, topped with crooked paper cones decorated with glittering foil stars. His mother has assembled his classmates. He doesn't think they're here to celebrate him. He just sees the inborn love of cake and party favors in their glowing faces. He always sees smiles.

His mother's face emerges from behind the flash. She stands at his side, all made up. Ribbons run red and blue coils through her brown hair; bright red lips part and reveal perfect white teeth. Her eyes look tired.

Other adults stand around the table, idling conversing through the sound of screaming children.

One woman puts a paper cup down on the table and leans close to him. "Happy birthday!" she squeals, her breath soured by the adult beverage in the gaudy children's cup. She slaps her own son's hand away as he reaches for it.

His mother: "What do we say to the nice lady?"

Him: "Thank you."

He's not looking at the woman. He's staring past her, outside the cocoon of good cheer. His father stands in the doorway, leaning against the jamb. He's just home from work, wearing a brown suit and five-o'clock shadow. The boy's eyes meet his and he sighs a quiet breath of resignation before turning away. Going back to his room. His chair.

The boy doesn't understand. Everyone else is happy. That's normal. But today, he thought his father might be too. He pushes his chair back rom the table and just then his mother pushes the swinging kitchen door open with her rear. She turns, revealing a flotilla of cupcakes, loaded with frosting and aglow with candles. Her teeth gleam orange in the candlelight, the spark of a single tear on tracing a bright line down her cheek.

Back on the bed, in the present, it's twenty-four years later. The boy — now man — wonders what he would have found had he followed his father. A man hiding? Defeated? He supposes it doesn't matter now. Time has passed, things have changed. Like time itself, he and his father have kept going. Always moving in the same direction.

Apart.

Graduation

Years ago.

The boy stood smiling for photographs, blue gown draped over his gangly frame. He had to keep adjusting the tassel that swung from the front of his cap. It was getting in his eyes, synthetic fibers tickling his nose. He stood at the front of a crowd assembled, and delivered a valedictory address.

"In closing, we should remember our time here. But be sure to move forward. Into the future. And with it, into our new selves."

It was clichéd, but the crowd erupted in applause and a cascade of camera flashes as he finished. His mother stood in the front, a broad smile emphasizing the lines she'd developed through years of happiness. His father clapped absentmindedly, going on a moment too early, then sitting down, embarrassed.

They announced the names and awards. He was head of the class. He'd been told for years that he was special, and had begun to believe in the myth of himself.

He would start that September at an Ivy League university. He'd been awarded a scholarship, would receive a full-ride to what otherwise would have crippled his family's income. Still, he felt he needed to do more.

He stepped down from the stage, having earned all his accolades and the piece of paper he would need. Many smoked cigars, though his mother wouldn't allow him to. He'd been a fragile child, asthma and allergies stealing much of his youthful health from him. But today, here and now, all was well. He was a success.

His father stood silently and watched his approach as his mother ran forward, throwing her arms around him and unleashing a belt of sobs into her son's bony shoulder. "Mom. Mom. It's okay," he pleaded. He looked around and was upset to see the scene being photographed. A grin on the face of a man with a camera strapped around his neck.

His father came forward and perfunctorily shook his hand, reaching past his mother's quivering back as though she wasn't there. He clasped his other strong hand on his son's elbow and simply said, "Well done. Well done. I'm going to get some refreshments." And with that, he was off.

They drove home in relative silence, occasionally punctuated by more of his mother's tears. She kept telling him she was just proud, but he could see and feel her breaking within. She was losing him.

He spent the summer working in a local bookstore, preparing for his new life to come in the fall. She deteriorated, growing alternately detached and clingy. His father was a constant though, an icy presence at his post in the living room. The day it came time to leave, his father woke early, shaved, dressed in his best suit and packed the car. All before anyone else was up. It was the first time the boy had seen the man look alive.

Letter From The Father: Year 20

Regret is to people what autumn is to leaves. It withers them, takes away what made them what they were. Leaving behind crooked husks.

She's dead.

She's gone and died.

After the boy left, the calls came further and further apart. He'd found a new life and she was left here, in the wreckage. Empty nest and all that. But this was worse. She was like an addict in withdrawal. Her face was taut leather over pointy bones, two ravenous eyes glaring at everything she'd come to hate in his absence. She didn't feel she'd wasted her life: she felt I'd wasted it for her. Letting him leave like that. Encouraging it. I thought it was the only nice thing I could do for the child. God knows I don't feel much love for him.

I'd always wondered what power that boy had over her. Whether it was simple psychology or something different. There was just a glimmer about him. Everyone seemed to see it. I remember thinking "What's the big deal?" I remember ignoring him. Punishing him in my vanity. Well, now she's gone. For good. That's probably punishment enough.

She'd been fading for 20 years now. But the end was sudden. Abrupt. Ugly. I took her to the hospital, as she hadn't been out of his room in days. I walked in and she was crouched on the floor like an animal, head resting on the foot of his bed. Her hair torn out in hanks, bits of it across the bedspread like patches of grass poking through the cracks in the sidewalk.

She turned and glared at me. I asked if she was coming out, was going to eat. Then the screaming started. I didn't know what to do. Called an ambulance, had her taken away on a stretcher.

I don't know if I feel guilty.

Before they closed the door, I heard the say thing I would ever hear her say. "This is all your fault." She spat it out at me, head reared back and gums showing like a wild animal caught in a corner.

I actually recoiled from it. Not from horror. Not from guilt. Just from the tone of it. I knew she'd changed. I knew she loved him and hated me. I had accepted it. Resigned myself. But to see it, to get confirmation: that was just too much.

They took her to the psych ward over at County. She was admitted — committed — whatever they call it. She got ahold of some cleaning products somehow. Managed to poison herself in the damned hospital. They found her the next day, toes and fingers curled in from the convulsions. I have to call the boy.

Maybe I should go visit. Do this right. In person. Maybe I owe him that.

Maybe he owes me something too.

I'll write again soon. I know it's been a long time, but it's been good to be back in touch with you. Correspond with someone who understands me, seems to care. I can't tell you how much I appreciate that.

Thank you.

Son's Memory

He still sometimes dreams of it. The day his father visited him. The day things changed. He sleeps, innocent and firmly tucked beneath sheet and quilt, and the visions come to him.

By the end, his face was a mess. Tears left thin salty tracks on his cheeks, his mouth dribbling with spit and rage. His father's face was the opposite: an austere landscape of desert-dry crinkles and a lightly grimacing mouth.

His father had surprised him. A month after starting his Junior year he was once again settling into dormitory life. He had begun to gather about him a cluster of new friends, a gaggle of new opinions about who he was and how the world worked. Reinventing himself for the umpteenth time since leaving home. And then the old man had to come and shatter all that. In the end, he thought the man hadn't been forced. He thought the old man had come specifically to devastate him.

The old man stood in the doorway, tweed cap in hand and tan jacket on, staring into the face of a stranger. The boy was tall now, and thin, tufts of wild brown hair and his mother's eyes. A long, sloping nose and pointed chin. Stark contrast to his father's strong jaw and glowering brown eyes.

"Can I come in, then?"

"Oh. Right. Yeah, of course."

The boy didn't know what to call this man. He supposed "Dad" was appropriate, but it just never came out naturally. He awkwardly stepped aside and shut the door behind him as his father surveyed his living quarters.

"Spacious. Quite nice. You share it, I assume?"

"Yeah. Roommate's just gone out. Had a date," he paused, trying to address the man directly, "Dad," he ventured, "Why are you here?"

The old man had recoiled slightly at the familial term. He spun to face the window, looking out over the moonlight grass of the quad, still littered with evidence of that day's relaxation. He sighed.

"I'm not sure how to tell you this," he began, lying, "Your mother's died."

There it was. Point-blank, no punches pulled. It hung in the air like the heat of a jungle, all pressure and smells and the occasional insect. He heard the boy began to stutter and blubber, a coffee pot beginning to percolate.

"Wh—What?"

"Your mother. She… she didn't do so well after you left. I didn't want to worry you," the old man was speaking through clenched teeth now, biting back a bitter smile, "She had to be hospitalized and… she didn't make it."

"Well what happened?!?" The boy's heart was pounding. He wanted to destroy the man before him, he wanted to kill him for his calm, for the clinical and patronizing way he was reciting the facts of his mother's death. But he couldn't make himself move. He was frozen, everything sped up. Thoughts came faster than the tongue could move, and possible action plans were all thwarted by the single, monolithic factor: the absence of his mother from this life.

"You don't need to know the details. I can tell you're very upset and we can speak about this later. I just thought you should know. Be told. In person." The last words came out a bit too harsh, as though proving what the boy already suspected. The old man was rubbing it in. If not enjoying it, at least getting some sense of recompense for what he viewed as the massive wrong of the boy's very existence.

"Tell... me." The words came out strained. The boy breathed deeply now, trying to relax himself.

"We can speak about this tomorrow. I'm staying in town."

"Tell me!" The boy shouted. His voice filled the room, and his fist reflexively shot out, slamming against the heavy wooden door. Numbing tingles of pain radiated up his arm, but he didn't care. The old man's eyes had widened at that.

"She took her own life. She had trouble with you leaving. She was so attached, and she didn't adjust well. They took her… to the hospital. She cursed me. Damned me. Somehow she got ahold of something, killed herself. Ended it. I guess life wasn't living without you." The last words dripped with cool venom.

"How can you not care? What did she do to you? Was she so awful?"

"You didn't see it, boy. You never could have. She forgot me. Forsook me. For you. From the day you came home, she doted on you, worshipped you. As though you were the key to her fucking happiness. As though you held all the answers she thought she'd found with me, when I was just a means to some other end. And that end was you. She thought you were special. They all fucking do.

"Look at you, here, in this hallowed hall of learning," his voice rich with sarcasm, he went on, spittle gathering at the corners of his mouth, "People kissing your ass night and day, telling you how special you are and how wonderful you are. Smiling at you, giving you A's, pats on the back, it's been your whole life. But what about me? I was nothing more than a sperm donor. You'll never understand how that feels. To be left behind, to be forgotten by someone who had loved you, who had promised to stay with you through thick and thin… In sickness and in fucking health. Well she left me for most of her health and came back in sickness only to tell me to go to hell! I'm worthless. I've been worthless your whole life. Whereas you bring happiness and glory wherever you go. I'm jealous of it. But more than that, every time I see you bring a smile to someone's face… every time I see happiness in your life, all I can think of is my mistakes."

It was the most the old man had ever said to the boy. They both realized this in the silence, as his words reverberated off thin walls. The old man was gasping, and suddenly appeared very small. He had let out all he'd held onto for the past 20 years. And now he was empty.

He gruffly repeated that he was staying in town and would see the boy in the morning. The boy stepped out of his way, quietly fuming. The heat of tears in his eyes and on his cheeks. The door opened, and the old man said over his shoulder, "You were her everything. That was too much responsibility for you to have. Good night."

The door closes, in his dreams. Only for the knocking to start so the whole thing can play out again and again. His feet twitch and his face contorts in the darkness, his head turning from side to side as though he could deny what he knew to have happened.

What he knew to be true.

Son's Memory, Part II

The next morning had yielded a quiet, stale breakfast. The food lay uneaten, cooling and congealing in heaps upon diner flatware. The old man spoke occasionally, remarking on the scenery of the campus and the presumption he held that his hard earned dollars were being put to good use. The son sulked and sweated, expending most of his energy to hold back rage and tears.

The old man left that day, patting the son once upon the shoulder — a minor contact but the first in years — before clambering into the wood paneled station wagon for the four-hour drive. The son returned to his room.

He sat on the edge of his bed, motionless. Memories ran before his eyes, finding their way out of the lines in the weave of the carpet. Her face. The eyes, smiling and wise as they teased him. Her head thrown back, laughing at his childish innocence. No more.

He knew there could be no more.

This was the knowledge that devastated him. He hadn't loved his mother, at least not in the conditional sense. He had relied on her. Taken her for granted. She had been an ever-ready presence in his life. She was there to defend him against all attackers, to protect him and coddle him and ultimately worship him. She had seen greatness in him, and he had borrowed that sight. Now he could see nothing for himself.

In retrospect, it was likely unhealthy. It was too much to bear, too close. Her love and adoration had been like a light shone directly into his eyes, causing twinges of pain in the corners of his skull and the sweat to bead upon his forehead.

She had pressured him.

Since arriving at college, he had had numerous women, each aligned with his particular political views of the day. The publicly uptight but privately filthy when he wore his blazer, Oxford blue shirt and khakis; the loose and tie-dyed unshaven when he wore torn pants and sunglasses in the evening. They had all served the same purpose. To support him. To allow him someone to feed off of in lieu of his own identity. To comment on his brilliance and give him light in which to flourish.

He had no sense of self. None. And in the stark, cold light of the morning, he felt it in his bones. He was just that. Bones and blood and skin, wandering through life, trying on new sets of ideals as someone switches fashions. He wondered if he could ever embrace it, the nothingness within.

Fill it with something useful, perhaps.

He wasn't sure. He stared long and hard at the corner of his roommate's bed, across the room from his own where he now perched. The roommate, asleep and oblivious, with a pending headache from the alcohol in his veins, stirred. He sat up, turned to his cohabitant, now perched on the icy precipice of adulthood, and asked, "What're you doing?"

"My mother. She's dead."

"Oh Jesus. Shit. I'm... Sorry." The words were stilted. Genuine shock mixed with a complete ignorance of how to handle such news.

"I think it's okay."

"Is there's anything I can do?"

At that the boy chuckled, a harsh sound mixed with the throatiness of a sob. "No. You're fine. Go back to sleep. I need to get out."

"Well just let me know," the roommate replied, already rolling over to sleep off a heavy night's partying.

"I will."

With that, the boy stood, standing on legs that quivered lightly beneath him. He felt as though he was floating, and before he knew it, he was out, bare toes spread amongst the stiff grass of a September afternoon. Staring up at the trees and brick corners of buildings. The sun showered his face with its light, as though smiling down warm kisses upon him.

Year 33. The Inevitable.

The boy is now a man. He stands, feet upon the pavement of a bustling Manhattan street. He is successful. He turned his nothingness into purpose, bringing to bear a wealth of skills and emotional detachment to the field his father had excelled in. A floor of a building in downtown New York now bears his name, and he serves on the board of an advertising agency. He makes decisions about what the rest of us want. He is a dream weaver, a craftsman of desires. He tells us what we need, and we obey, without question.

Some time ago, he wed a bright young woman, herself poised as the fashion iconoclast of the 21st century. Together they would rule, serving twin roles as the other's muse, determining the course of American culture and the future of taste.

Things at home are not going well.

She has found solace in the arms of another. A striking young model 23 years of age. The model has not only made him a cuckold, but is about to make her a mother. They play it off, of course. Pose as the happy couple when cameras demand it. He finds his own comfort in the bottom of a bottle.

The man stands squinting into the sun, thinking of the feeling of grass between his bare toes. He misses those days of college, of innocence. The days he still feels his father stole.

His father is in a home now. His mind and body failed quickly in old age, retirement stealing what vitality he had remaining. His lungs filled with fluid, his brain became increasingly unreliable. It's now been four years since he began his slow decline into obsolescence, function after function being stolen from him. And it's been three years since the man went to see him. To bear witness to the decline. After a while, the vengeance came too slowly. The old man simply wasn't dying fast enough to satisfy his son: a disappointment as always.

The son stands on the corner, and he thinks. Thinks of his father, thinks of the silent home in which he grew. Thinks of that visit, now over a decade ago, when the old man had arrived and shattered his soul as though it was nothing. It wasn't the loss of a loved one. It was as though someone had pulled the floorboards themselves out from under him. He lost his footing. Lost his grounding. Spun downward into uncertainty and mindlessness. He had wandered through the dark recesses of his own psyche, finding here and there the tattered remains of childhood happiness. Remembering the seeming magic of his own smile.

It had been years since a sincere smile had crossed his face. They just never came anymore. Even in his wedding photos, he had borne a forced wince, exposing the whites of his perfect teeth to reflect the camera's flash.

But here he stands. A sunny morning in the fall, feeling the comfortable breeze passing through his silken suit as the warm light caresses his upturned face. The light before him turns from a white silhouette of a walking man to a flashing red hand, and he feels tears in his eyes. He thinks of his wife, of the growing betrayal in her body. Of the physical beauty the model father will have given to their child. Something he himself could never give. He hasn't felt this pure, this happy in years. Their dishonesty has freed him.

A smile teases at the corner of his mouth as the red hand materializes and stays. A stern warning.

His lips part and the beam shines forth: his unadulterated happiness for all to see. He is finally free. Finally empty. No attachments. No responsibility. He forgets work, forgives the cheating bitch he's married. Forgets the shadow of his father, wasting away in a room that smells of disinfectant.

The toes of his six hundred dollar shoe hang off the curb as cars rush past.

Tourists on either side of him chatter about Ground Zero, about life and about the majesty of the city.

He wonders, idly, if they know who he is. Probably not.

His right foot lifts. Another car rushes by, a taxi with a camera sticking out of the window, snapping pictures of a famous skyline from a useless perspective.

The smile on his face broadens, and he steps off the curb. The tourists, unknowing, basking in the happiness finally released from the prison of his self-control, step forth in unison.

The cars rush towards them, an unruly chorus of horns blaring atonally into the sunny sky. Brakes squeal.

In the end, it's all ruled an accident. And no one is there to correct that.

VIII

Me in the World: Complaining About 60 Cycle Hum in the Land of the Deaf

*I could strip nude
And run through Grand Central Station
And bellow all the ills of the world
Straight into their rounded faces.
And they might smile,
And reach for a camera.
And think "What a show we wandered into."*

Open Letter.

Ladies and Gentlemen of the Internet age,

It is important to note, firstly, that by the standards traditionally held to, none of you are ladies or gentlemen. If you were, you would not be on the Internet. Even if you are online only to check in on your Internet book club or a forum that discusses a common interest, you are the next-door neighbor of depravity. Of insanity.

The Internet gives us each a mouthpiece, a megaphone. The sick, twisted soul who would have watched a film loop of an execution in the 1970s– That kid you knew in high school who couldn't get enough Faces of Death–now has a bullhorn. He can blast your mind irrevocably with little more than a hosting site and your innocent click on a triangular play button.

Exercise caution. For here there be monsters.

Desensitization is but one pitfall. Vicarious

trauma from bearing witness to international murder. The loss of innocence in a child trained to murder for Mexican drug cartels drains you of what little purity you may have left. Witnessing the glistening bodies of people who fornicate like trained beasts, caricatures of human sexuality, may render you febrile, insecure over the weight you carry in the wrong places.

We are all inundated with information. Our minds fill throughout the day, and we go into withdrawal without that flood of new knowledge. We crave it, and we hate it all the same.

That is the Internet. That is the future. And oddly, that has been the past as well. Society has always been simultaneously participated in and rebelled against. Everything accelerates, but nothing essentially changes. The net we cast into the seas of the world grows bigger, but the winch we use to reap our haul grows stronger.

I have mixed feelings about you, Internet. A force of empowerment, and one of corruption and foulness.

I just thought I should share that with you. Get it all out on the table. So we can know where we stand.

April 1st and The Internet: Trouble In Paradise

Like so many other people, I assume the golden age of pranking to be the 1890 s. I mean think about it: the gullibility of man as demonstrated by snake oil salesman and the dubious invention of soft drinks as medicine, the advent of electricity (which opened new doors in pranking technology), and the simultaneous love for and suspicion of all things new and spectacular.

Which brings me to my point: The Internet has ruined April Fool's Day. It used to be that people only received so much information at one time. The local paper, a friend with a hilarious waxed mustache, etc. Nowadays, we are inundated. My RSS feeds, while likely not over-subscribed or impressive, still manages to kick up 200-300 new items per day. And today, of those, I basically refused to believe all of them that were not hilarious photographs of people falling and/or adorable animals. Why?

Because it's April 1st. A day when the Internet is flooded with false news stories. From rumors of celebrity demises to Google changing its name to

Topeka, the Internet becomes slightly less easy to navigate and definitely more irritating. Of course, this brings forth the larger issue of whether or not we should be this skeptical of internet reporting at all times. I think we should. But I think we don't want to. Or at least I don't want to. It's a hassle, analyzing it, and by the time you reach the items that are most definitely jokes, you feel tired and irritated. It's like a toddler jumping out from behind a corner and yelling boo. The first time, he might surprise you. The second, it's still cute. By the 50th, you just want to tell him that it doesn't work anymore, and you wish he would go somewhere else for a while.

Oh, and before anyone even considers it, I don't understand why Rick Astley is a joke. He has a lovely voice.

Letter From The Front: Groceries and Bad Attitudes

I just ventured out into the world briefly, to acquire vegetables for tonight's dinner. Tired of seeing the moldy clementines and flaccid celery Stop and Shop has to offer, I thought that I would brave the Prius-driving hordes of 40-something first-time moms and go to Whole Foods. The produce is good, it's clean, organized, and there aren't those mysterious piles of discarded individual leaves of lettuce. Sure, you pay more, but who cares.

I collected what I needed to manufacture a capable meatloaf, mashed root vegetables and cooked-down greens. A healthy, albeit old-fashioned spread that I hope to enjoy in a few hours. But it was what occurred at the checkout that resonated with me.

I walked up to the express checkout line, 10 items or less being a category I fit fairly well with my meager ingredients, and waited patiently as the two people in front of me had their items rang up. As the woman in front of me passed her items over the counter, I saw that she was buying two containers of blueberries, one of strawberries and heavy cream. The cashier and another employee (who was bagging the items) chatted playfully, she chiding him for some unknown offense. Suddenly the berry-buyer was irritated. "Come on," she intoned, sounding disappointed more than anything else, "Hurry it up. You've got work to do to, honey." Long pause as the cashier typed on the cash register and gave this woman her total. "You can socialize after work."

The woman's face was a sagging, painted scowl. Her hair a perfect helmet of dyed red, that color that woman begin to accept as "natural" looking the later into life they get. She continued to sigh loudly and groan even as the cashier handed her her receipt and change.

I purchased my items and commented to the cashier how rude that woman had been. "It's alright," she said, "I'm used to it." I thought about my experience navigating the store. I had dodged several carts, piloted by absent-minded women texting on blackberries and iPhones. I had been bumped into by a woman in search of the perfect shiitake mushroom, and narrowly dodged the elbow of some well-intentioned locavore reaching for something atop a high shelf.

Suddenly I wanted to chide this woman, this foul creature, who had criticized someone for enjoying themselves at work. I had wanted to say something in the moment, but had apparently lacked words. I wanted to point out how childish and rude she was, how she wouldn't lose any time from her busy day of buying out-of-season fruit and driving about in what I assume is a tank labeled "BMW" or "Lexus" because two people enjoyed themselves while serving her. Point out how getting worked up over little things like this led to the release of stress hormones that might well be responsible for her burgeoning paunch and the tightness of her gold rings on her stubby, bloated fingers.

But in the moment, when it was happening, I

had only one thought. "What a cunt."

Perhaps her negativity and my emotional reaction to it had clouded my normally decent abilities for analysis and response. Perhaps I was just blind-sided by this flagrant, public display of rudeness. I think it must have been okay in her head for one of several reasons. Entitlement is the most basic. The sense of "I am paying. You will serve me" that we all fall prey to now and again. Dig deeper and I would bet you would find a well-to-do woman of her generation feeling very little control over their lives. Dig even deeper and you might just find racism (the cashier was Hispanic, the coworker black).

But I'm over analyzing now. Frankly, it would have been better just to say she was being a cunt. She would have gotten a shock, I could have purged my head of the negative thought that her ludicrous behavior had put there, and I would have looked like a hero of the working class to those poor peddlers of carefully sourced organic produce and bacteria/sea kelp/rotten milk disguised as food.

But that's how it is. You never can think of the right thing in the moment. You can only sigh, roll your eyes when the woman is out of sight, and move on with your day. Do your best not to let the petty squabbles of others pollute your mind.

And then, of course, go home and enjoy your dinner. Because that woman, even buying luxurious out-of-season produce that it took the exploitation of several groups of people to get to her, will go home and stuff her face, looking for the next fight.

Groceries Part II: Clean-Up, Aisle Humanity

I peer down the crowded rows of cashiers, attempting to spy an open self-checkout. Technology allows us to minimalize the amount of human contact we have in places of commerce, and I for one embrace it. I spot a man fumbling with the automated payment system, and assume he'll be quick to move. There's no line behind him. In the future that will be read as a warning, but for now I slip into place behind him. The unfortunately purple plastic basket containing yogurt, milk and a Diet Pepsi weighs heavily in the crook of my left elbow.

The man is 40 or so, dressed in clothing too young. He wears girlish-cut black jeans, the back pockets sagging from his lack of buttock. Above he is clad in a slightly-too-tight black and gray striped sweatshirt, glasses on his face with thick plastic frames. He looks a bit like a like a puzzled Armenian frog, I think to myself. The machine implores him, in its garbled techno-voice, to "Use the electronic pen to sign the signature tablet." He stares mutely at the card-swipe apparatus, apparently oblivious to the small glowing area below.

I wait a beat, then two. Then, with my heart fluttering in preparation for discomfort, I make a small grunting/coughing sound to get him to look up and gesture with my free hand. "That one." It comes out too loudly, too resonantly. Like a command, not a helpful suggestion. He must know I don't want to be here.

"Oh." He says dumbly. I attempt to smooth it over, continuing, "Yeah. It can be confusing. Half the time nothing shows up on there." He mutters a word that might be "Thanks" and waits for his receipt. As he moves down to bag his groceries, which I see to be Soy Milk and some sort of lo-fat ultra-health frozen dessert, I continue, with no idea why I'm talking. "It's a flawed system. One day…" I leave it there.

He looks up, suddenly, his bug-eyes cutting a line straight to my face, which I'm hoping looks friendly at this point. "Thanks for your help." He says it tersely, with the expression one normally reserves for bad milk. You know the one, the one you see right before the person asks you to smell this, even though they know it's bad.

He grabs his groceries and walks off in what is either a rush or a huff.

Was I just an asshole? I think this to myself as I scan 4 yogurts and a carton of milk. I also consider whether or not he was offended by my apparent dairy consumption, in the face of his soymilk. Lactose tolerance envy? Note to self: Google that later.

I end up deciding it doesn't really matter whether or not I was an asshole. Whether or not a stranger likes me is ultimately of no importance whatsoever. But still, I feel that tickle in the back of my head. The faint hint of embarrassment and shame. And I resolve to go home and write it down before I lose touch with that painfully human sensation.

Media And Consumerism in a World of Violently Competing –Isms.

I recently did a monthly wander through a bookstore, and realized something. In the bit near the front, you know, the "Shit it really seems like you ought to read" section? Anyway, in that bit, there was a row of books, alternating arguments for and against God. The "God Delusion" begets "The Case for the Divine" begets "Atheists are Right" begets "FUCK YOU, GOD'S THERE." Those aren't exact titles, but that progression does pretty accurately represent the increasing impoliteness of what is fast becoming America's biggest polemic industry.

My own feelings on the nature of the divine are both complex and not really worth discussing here. But I will say this. I feel as though the amount of effort and energy being put forth trying to convince the other side is… well, wasteful. Certainly for those who purport to be believers. I find it difficult to argue with atheists writing these books, because they seem to spend most of their time loudly displaying their atheism anyways, be it at a bar, coffee shop, or christening. Most people who are evangelical atheists (won't that term just make their skin crawl?) are basically assholes anyways, and since there is no God in their worldview, they don't have better God-related things to do with their time. The pro-Godders, on the other hand... It seems like not every one of these Atheistic tomes needs a response. Surely God would prefer you do something a bit more interesting with your time than talk about why, according to the insufferably tight quarters of human logic, He/She/It actually IS. If you believe in God, you must assume God to have some form of awareness of God's own existence, so you certainly aren't writing the book for God's benefit. Right? So why not go out and instead do all the nice things God historically seems to have told people to do, instead of wasting paper and time and breath arguing with people who, if they are right, will be worm food for eternity anyways? Life's too short.

Oh, caveat to the "Do things God historically

seems to have told people to do": I meant in terms of charity, good works, and such. Not so much crusades, jihads, or anything the Norse or Greek gods told people to do. They were just creepy. For proof, see Odin, king of the Aesir, the race of Norse gods. He cut out his eye and threw it down a well to gain insight into future, then hanged himself from the tree of life. What was he so curious about in the future? His own death. Ragnarok. The End of all things.

That is a god I wouldn't want to meet in a dark alley.

D.R.E.A.M. (Death Rules Everything Around Me)

Ghost Adventures.

Yes, I will be discussing Travel Channel's horrendous ode to the frat-boy paranormal. Effectively, the show consists of three men who lock themselves in spooky and purportedly haunted houses, prisons and shutdown hospitals with infrared cameras and other wacky devices in an attempt to document something from beyond. I'm going to let you, the reader, imagine that "the beyond" was read by Vincent Price with a shitload of reverb.

Now, I got into this show during the pre-Halloween marathons of scary nonsense that floods our televisions every year. This is, for the record, one of my favorite times of the year. I had nothing much to do and was likely also writing on the computer, and in the background, I heard the following exchange.

Allow me to set the scene. The large muscle-bound fellow who leads the three men sits in a chair on a plantation. A haunted plantation, specifically, in Louisiana, that is apparently riddled with Voodoo curses. He claims to feel something scratch him. Immediately he shouts to his tech-nerd buddy, whom he addresses solely as "bro." "Bro! Come here, bro! Sit in this chair. I felt something, bro, I felt something!"

"Bro" complies, and they trade places. As the poor guy-who-knows-how-to-work-the-camera sits in a chair, in the former hospital of this plantation, where God only knows how many slaves met a horrid end, the muscle-bound leader begins to yell: "Show yourself. Show him what you showed me. Show him you're here! Unless you're chicken!" or something to that effect.

Bro becomes uncomfortable. Bro makes a case: "What did the guy tell us? What was the first rule?!? Don't taunt voodoo, man! Don't taunt voodoo!"

Musclehead, a faux-hawked pile of man in a super-tight shirt named Zak Bagans, retorts: "I'm not taunting voodoo."

Bro, whose name is apparently Aaron, speaks the sentence that seals my fate as a lifetime fan: ***"You are taunting the crap out of voodoo right now, bro."***

I nearly died laughing. I nearly gave up my proverbial ghost, clutching at my sides and wincing as the sheer ludicrousness of this situation rolled over me. Waves of delirium tickled my fancy, and I was once again struck by how improbable most television is.

It was magic.

On The More General Subject of Paranormality.

I'm conflicted, frankly, on the entire subject. I feel a rational portion of me that sees man as machine. A sort of Cartesian dualism crammed into my head by a Western upbringing screams, "The ghost is gone! The machine breaks down!" Then there is a part of me that desperately wants there to be something more, if only to avoid the inevitable scrap-yarding of my bodily self without being able to go onto something else.

Aside: There are several people I would love to haunt.

At any rate, the intense desire to believe in something is a tricky thing, as it tends to make us more willing to invent evidence. I watch Ghost Adventures and see men in the dark being frightened by houses settling, claiming echoes of their own voice (when cleverly "enhanced") are voices from beyond the grave. It's nonsense. It's entertainment. But there are lots of other stories.

In addition to the threatening ghosts we think of as tormenting people, there is hearsay evidence from my late grandfather, who informed me the last time I saw him that there was a man who sometimes appeared in the doorway of his bedroom. His theory about it was unique. He didn't believe that the man was there to threaten him, or even because of unfinished business. In what seemed crazy at the time but seems brilliant the longer I think about it, he said this: "You know how places change you? How you remember things? I think maybe we change places. They remember us."

I love that thought.

IX

The Truth as I Have Come to Understand It

*And so we've reached the bottom.
The sky so far from here
Stars are nothing but pinpricks
Clouds cobwebs
In the warmth and in the dank
Everything becomes close.
Within striking distance.
When you can touch it
Everything is true
And being is the all.*

Scraping The Bottom Of The Barrel

Surely each generation must sense it, but I feel myself a lonely pioneer. I come from a thin slice of the population, sandwiched between the snot-nosed Generation X and the somehow-even-snottier-nosed Millennials. The Internet came to me in adolescence, and the entertainment megacomplex of television, film and music has had its ugly talons in me from day one.

I am a media guinea pig.

I tend to take a dim view of all humanity. I am harshest, however, on myself. I see myself as a good intellect, perhaps in certain circumstances a great one, but with drawbacks that I see as endemic in my population.

I am a genius without character.

I don't mean that I am some kind of devious supervillain. Perhaps that would be better, or at least more interesting. What I mean is that I have intellectual abilities and opportunities that my parents could only have dreamt of, from pre-natal exposure to classical music to flash cards and readings before kindergarten. I am laden with cognitive skills. But exist without work ethic. I have never stared down the barrel of a real honest hard day's labor, nor been accountable for the source of my next meal.

And now what am I but a dilettante? An overgrown child pretending adulthood, pretending creativity, pretending taste and discernment.

All is pretense in the 21st century.
I am a polymath, but not out of brilliance. Rather my diverse interests stem from something that was clumsily labeled "attention deficit," as though attention was something one comes filled with and knows how to deploy at any moment without cue or guidance.

I was trained to know better.

Trained to feel above authority figures who likely could have whipped me into shape, if they dared to buck the self-esteem industry. I was trained only to heed those who came kowtowing to me, offering trophies and awards for mere participation. All in the name of self-worth. A sense of competence. Each of us being more special than the last and the next. We were all unique, sparkling gems: individuals in the worst way possible.

Without community. Culture. Decency.

How do I regain humility I never had, when I was taught to think of it as self-hatred? Accountability when it was defined as self-doubt and negativity.

How do I find meaning in a world I am so accustomed to distrusting? Can there be a substitute for the cynicism and skepticism I have taken beyond the boundaries of sense and good taste?

Who knows?

Who, perhaps, cares?

The adults of my youth, now late in life, have realized their mistakes. They have chosen to implement school programs to teach grit and character, leadership and self-starterdom. But that is now. They've elected to fix the next generation.

In the end, this leaves me floating onwards, rudderless and brilliant. Perfect to so many, but in my dark and empty heart, knowing the true depth of my flaws.

Disconnection

I close my eyes at night. There's no peace. There's blackness, and then background noises, like a broken TV that still had working speakers. So I sit in the dark, and I try to breathe, and I try to think. Clear, individual thoughts. It doesn't happen. I get a jumble. I get strange sensations in my body. I get floating, I get heavy. I get hot. Still.

And I begin to speak, with my eyes closed. I begin to think out loud and wonder what the hell I'm doing. I imagine scenarios that might never happen. I play through them, try to figure out what sort of emotion I would feel and how I would act. How my face would change. Or my voice.

Maybe the problem is that I'm so disconnected from how I actually feel that there exists this need to rehearse, and to artificially instill some sense of pathos in my own life.

I start to look at things unrealistically. I start to decide that what I should be doing is not remotely what I am, and that there's some perfect performance that I could give. That I could render a portrayal of a human being convincing enough that it would persuade people that nothing was wrong. That everything was normal.

And if I could persuade enough people — make it a tenet of their beliefs about me — that I could make it the way I see myself.

I assume, for the most part, that normality, insanity, art and obscenity all fall under that dubious characterization of knowing-it-when-one-sees-it.

Smiling children. A couple, screaming and laughing as the first drops of rain fall and they try to run inside. People making meaningful eye contact, shaking hands, doing deals. Putting on the same costume every day and going to work at the same job. Playing the same role every single day.

Normal is some combination of routine and connection. If you don't have a routine, you can't have replication. Normal thrives on replication and predictability. Normal requires your subservience to some great inherent agreed-upon structure, which may or may not be a projection. Regardless, it is of tremendous importance that it appears inherent.

The trouble is that anyone can be routinized. Anyone could join the military—provided they meet the requirements—and within weeks they would have a routine. Set. Possibly for the rest of his or her life. Connection, on the other hand, is much more difficult.

Connection exists between humans; it is built by communities, participated in and witnessed simultaneously. Like running a race, keeping time, and watching the changing colors of flags all at once. It's complex.

The rewards: participating in effervescence, going to events. Yet these require openness, and openness does not come naturally to all. At least not to me.

Openness — intimacy — does not occur for the most part in nature. The closest metaphoric analog I can think of is a beta dog bearing its throat in submission to the alpha. After the two dogs fight and one is clearly defeated, the loser cranes its head back, exposing the vulnerable lifelines of its throat and hoping to be spared. The alpha, being merciful but more so pragmatic, requires betas, gammas, all the way down the line, and decides that he will spare this dog. That is openness, and it requires of me that I trust my fellow man to spare me. Every single day. For life.

That they will allow me the room to exist. To simply be. They will respect and recognize my existence, and allow me to continue it, unmolested, or at the very least un-interacted with.

Normal: the bones of a giant. Perhaps we are cells. A body built of individuals working in concert, in routines of homeostasis and autonomic activities. Right now I feel more like a cancer. Changing shape, mutating, bucking the rules. I look for room to expand. Perhaps I grow. Perhaps I am stagnating.

One of the advantages of being an outside is the ability to decide who and what you wish to be to people. I feel faced with this decision in each and every interaction. That's what this noise in my head is, at night.

I'm faced with these options, one of which must be selected. The speeches I could give if I could only muster the courage to lie on my back, the supplicant dog, and bear my throat. To my elders, my betters, my loved ones.

Will they spare me?

My head says yes. Everything else whispers no. The tightness in my chest is a constant reminder of no. The tension of my shoulders forces my head forward, covering the soft tissues and vital portions of my throat. Denying not only the risk but even the metaphor I so sheepishly outlined herein.

When I walk the streets, when I see strangers or those I've known for years, a noise can startle me. The littlest thing. My hands ball into fists; my feet tingle with the urge to start running.

The desire to escape is itself a prison. This is where the panic sets in, but the panic is merely a symptom. A symptom of the disconnect between myself and the rest of the world. The deconstruction of normal relationships. I honestly don't know when it happened. It may not be important. All I know is that in the dark, in the small quiet hours, I am faced with the consequences of that break. And that itself is enough to bring on the waves of fear. The terrifying idea that normal may never exist for me, and that this prison inside my head is an endless, unsolvable maze.

The Truth

In the 21st century, when snark rules all, it seems that enjoyment is equated with stupidity. To smile is to show weakness. To enjoy things without irony is to unveil yourself as a hapless sheep, floating along a constantly gyrating stream of proscriptive norms that the "intelligent" folk have learned to avoid. Or at least swim upstream through, jeering and gibing their way across rocks of popular culture and normal life.

This is at once sad and dangerous. These affected blasé and ennui—and probably other French terms—individuals miss a great deal in their daily life. And engage in one of the most devastating phenomena: downward social comparison. The American Dream, in its classical sense, is to look at your neighbor who has things that are better than yours and aspire to those. Instead, we now look upon those who engage in things we think trivial and meaningless and mock them. We have become not a society of scrappy have-nots desirous of bettering ourselves; but rather a group of self-professed haves. We know the truth. And we're better than you for it.

I am here to admit that I have no idea what the truth is. To admit that the best I can do is some vague approximation of the thing itself, which may or may not exist. The truth, as I have come to understand it, is that most things are subjective. When viewed objectively, they are the proverbial mare's nest. There is either nothing there, or what is there is so very convoluted and difficult that it cannot be fully grasped. The only tenable position is to maintain an open mind. To give things a chance.

I believe we must attempt to enjoy, attempt to understand. It's nobler by far to resist the impulse to shit on something that you do not understand. To forcibly shake yourself from your set path.

We all live in ruts. The least we could do is look around from time to time and try to increase the erosion on one side or the other. We may never escape, but we could widen the track we've ended up with.

Debates of politics, atheism versus faith, food preferences, cultural happenings... All of these things are not black and white. They are in fact shockingly subtle gradients. There are few things one can know to be true. Other than it is possible to change one's mind about anything.

As the Internet and its various offshoots of mass communication apparati give us each a voice and a stump from which to orate, perhaps we should keep this in mind. Bear in mind that while you are typing your horrid comments, there are bots — not the robots imagined in the horrors and sci-fi of long ago, but rather more devious spiders made of ones and zeroes. These robots crawl across cyberspace, collecting and backing up data. Everything you've ever said. Everyone you've ever searched for. All that you are, per the modern definition of public discourse.

The modern day American Dream is one of having the knowledge that you have gotten the better of other individuals. Knowledge that your perceived competition has been bested.

But what is the actual victory? I for one have engaged in this many times, and have never left the keyboard feeling better about myself. Generally there is just a vague sense that I am still angry and empty and wishing I could have done more.

That may be the most insidious part of downward social comparison: it's addictive. Very much so. To give up insulting, shoring yourself up through reducing others… That makes the DTs look like a walk in the park. Emotionally, at least.

At times I wonder if there will need to be a rehabilitation center for it. There have already been rumors of Internet addiction treatment centers, but this particular phenomenon might not have been nailed down yet. So, in this, the final portion of this collection of my ranting and raving, I ask you to lay down your proverbial arms and attempt a different stratagem.

The truth about life is simple. Do what you want, don't hurt other people, and work hard. It took me 31 years to learn this. I spent years not doing what I wanted and that led to depression, anxiety, substance abuse, and general malaise. I spent many years hurting other people. Emotionally, physically, and generally. I sometimes catch myself reliving these experiences in my head. Catch myself on the cusp of an apology I never made but feel I should have. I feel deep shame and remorse over things that I'm sure other people don't think about.

Maybe that's just me.

To the last point, working hard. This book has been more work than I am accustomed to, and I love it for that. To have a physical product of your energies, that is a greatly satisfying feeling. I only wish I had done something like this ages ago.

Created something. Because work is not about doing what the boss says, or punching a clock, or making money. Work, in the sense that it applies to the truth about life, is about pursuing a goal. A goal that you yourself set. A goal that only you know the boundaries and requirements of, and then doing everything you can to reach it.

School attempts to instill this with gold stars and grades, parents with rewards and encouragement. But ultimately, as with all things. It must come from within. Because that is all we know, not to be overly solipsistic.

The truth, as I have come to understand it, is that it is more important to feel accomplished than it is to feel useful. To feel productive rather than to feel just competent.

To feel human, rather than mechanical.

And that should just about be the most honest thing I write down herein. Seems as good a place as any to end. Go be human.

Acknowledgements

As this process took quite some time, although most of it unconscious, there are many people who I wish to thank for their participation in this book. Admittedly the majority of them did so without really being aware, but every time I read them a line or emailed them something I thought was worth dealing with, or called them late at night to read them some super depressing essay on the subject of my self… That counts. So thus I must offer my most heartfelt thanks to the following individuals: Rachel, first and foremost, for her stalwart encouragement while having plenty on her own plate. Both Eds, who I won't print the last names of, who have been encouraging beyond belief. Dave and Lisa, whose general willingness to listen and unequivocal support has shored up my fragile ego on many more than one occasion. Taylor, who I lived with for a time during this entire process and put up with more than she should have, and then the various and sundry humans who provided more support: Charlie (for helping with the cover design process), Jim (clicking "like" on Facebook just about every time I posted something I thought was good), Sacha and Nora (unbounded enthusiasm and congratulations), Annie (for allowing space for my rage and reason alike), my family (who seemed vaguely interested and perhaps puzzled by my decision to do this, but supportive nonetheless) and lastly, and perhaps most importantly, me.

Yeah that's right. I thanked myself. Now that I'm a big fancy writer I can do that.

Please dear God let that be viewed as a joke, because that's how intended it. Seriously though, the most important individual in all of this is you. The person sitting there, holding this book or Kindle-esque device and thinking "Where the hell is he going with this?"

I'll give you a hint. I've already started something else. Look for it soonish. Or follow up for details on RichCresswell.com.

Thanks so much, and until next time.

-RJC-

Made in the USA
Lexington, KY
28 September 2013